Lethal
RETRACTION

DOBI CROSS

Luxhaven
Publishing

ISBN paperback, 978-1-958987-13-1

Interior & Cover Design by Luxhaven Publishing

Editing by JD Book Services

Proofreading by Lisa Lee Proofreading

To JC, Grandma D, and DC, whom I love more than life itself.

READ MORE BY DOBI CROSS

Dr. Zora Smyth Medical Thriller Series

Lethal Emergency (Prequel)

Lethal Dissection

Lethal Incision

Lethal Obsession

Lethal Reconciliation

Lethal Adhesion

Lethal Retraction

SEE ALL OF DOBI CROSS BOOKS

at https://dobicross.com

AUTHOR'S NOTE

Thank you for choosing **LETHAL RETRACTION**. Zora Smyth was a character I was fortunate to meet about two years ago as I brainstormed ideas for my first medical thriller story for an anthology.

LETHAL RETRACTION completes the story of Dr. Zora Smyth as she fights to finish up her fellowship and spend time with the people that matter the most to her. We see how Zora remains true to believing in herself and her dreams, while keeping trust with her friends and family.

It's still hard to believe that this series has come to an end, though we begin a new journey with Zora Smyth and Jason Martin in the next spin off series. I've enjoyed getting to know Zora, and I hope you've had fun too. A dear reader of mine called her "the world's unluckiest heroine," but I think she now has a richer and more meaningful life, and has ended up a much stronger person, able to take on anything in the world.

It was important for me as I penned this series to have Zora Smyth not be some super hero or a person with extraordinary abilities, but an everyday person who through the journey of the next few books comes to fully understand and appreciate who she truly is and is able to heal from the childhood baggage she's carried all her life.

Please continue this journey with me in the first book of the new spin off series, THE DOCTOR SPY, featuring both Dr. Jason Martin and Dr. Zora Smyth. You can grab your copy at https://dobicross.com.

Would you also want to be notified when the next Dobi Cross book releases? Sign up at https://dobi-cross.com.

Once again, thank you so much for purchasing LETHAL RETRACTION and for meeting Zora

Smyth. If you enjoyed it, please consider leaving a review at your favorite retailer or recommending it to a friend.

Thanks again for your support!

Dobi Cross

Lethal
RETRACTION

The night stood still, the air ominous, when the two men arrived in the shadowed parking lot.

"Are you sure this is the car?" Tommy asked, gesturing to the grey sedan in front of them. People sometimes described him as the muscle with the flat forehead.

The shorter man in the oversized black coat had the unusual name—considering he looked or acted nothing like the original—of Elvis. He sighed as if about to instruct a five-year-old on the importance of toilet paper after using the loo. "It's parked in the corner lot like the boss said it would be. Have I ever been wrong?"

Well, you have, Tommy thought to himself. But

this was not the time to point it out. They'd arrived late to the lot, the first part of the job having taken longer than expected, and now the cover of darkness they'd needed was already making way for dawn. From the moment the boss had given him the assignment, something about it hadn't sat right with him, and now all Tommy wanted was to be done with it. He adjusted his stance to hold the package they carried together with one hand, then he thrust his other hand into his jacket and pulled out a device.

"You remember how to use it, right?" Elvis asked.

I'm not that stupid, Tommy thought, though his mind got scrambled sometimes. But Boss hadn't hired him for his brains, and he could leave all the thinking to him, or her—Tommy wasn't sure who Boss was, since he dressed like a man and spoke like a woman. It didn't matter though—Boss's knife was just as deadly and didn't discriminate. All Tommy had to do was obey whatever instructions Boss gave him. Boss had said the device was some sort of repeater, whatever that meant, and would get the job done.

He pointed the device at the car and pressed the big red button like he'd been told to do.

The trunk popped open like magic.

Tommy's jaw dropped. There hadn't even been an alarm blare, like he'd been expecting. Tommy had seen nothing like it.

"Ah. Nice. I should get one of these for myself," Elvis said. "We'll be rich in no time."

True. Stealing cars and selling them to the chop shops would be easy-peasy with this. But Tommy and Elvis would also end up at the bottom of the river as fish food if Boss had anything to say about it—he was protective of his stuff that way.

The area darkened, and an uneasiness crept over Tommy. He shivered, and his eyes darted around in search of what might have caused the change, but he found nothing except empty cars dead to the world until their owners turned the key. Then he remembered how he'd felt about the job, and all he wanted was to be far away from here as soon as possible. "We need to hurry," he said to Elvis.

They dropped the package and it landed in the open trunk with a loud *thump*. As expected, no blood escaped into the carpeted space from the cellophane-wrapped body, since Tommy and Elvis had perfected the act of wrapping up a body as if it was luggage about to be rolled into a plane's underbelly. Then Tommy slammed the trunk shut.

His job here was done. Now it was up to the

cleaners to do the rest. Tommy had learned not to be curious about why Boss chopped up some bodies into parts and dumped them in the river, while others got passed to the cleaners. He wasn't like Elvis trying to know everything—Tommy had learned that remaining ignorant was the best way to keep his head on his shoulders.

The darkness of the night faded, warning Tommy that it was time to disappear. He removed the gloves he wore, tucked them into the deep recesses of his jacket, and jumped into the van they'd parked nearby. Elvis did the same.

Then Tommy drove through the rows of parked cars, past the open gate, and joined the throng of highway commuters headed back into the city.

2

Someone crashed into her shoulder from behind, and Dr. Zora Smyth stumbled and landed on one knee just as she'd stepped off the escalator.

Pain shot through her body. *Ouch!* The hand luggage she'd been carrying skittered away, landing a few feet ahead.

She glared at the culprit, who'd hurried ahead without stopping in the almost empty sunlit terminal, a black hoodie obscuring his features. *What is wrong with people these days? This guy didn't even bother to apologize.*

Then the last thing she'd expected happened.

The assailant crashed to the ground like something had hit him. Yet Zora couldn't see what had halted his escape. Instead, the guy hurried to his feet and limped away as fast as he could, but he'd left a pink and purple item on the floor where he'd been kneeling only a second ago.

Zora's eyes widened, and she patted her jacket. Yes, that was indeed her wallet lying on the floor! She hadn't even noticed it was missing.

She'd rewarded herself with the custom purple and pink wallet from one of her favorite designers after passing the exams that made her a board-certified general surgeon two months ago. Matter of fact, she was returning from her first conference since she'd achieved the new status. Zora had met old friends and made new connections in the week she'd spent in Europe, and it had been a great time to catch up with everyone. She'd even gotten some new research ideas and was keen to get back and start working on them. One of those ideas had been on her mind when the assailant had bumped into her.

She rose to her feet and was about to rush over to where the wallet lay, when a man in a tan trench coat picked it up, stepped over to where her luggage had landed, and grabbed it too. Then he strode over with both items to where she stood.

"I believe these are yours," he said with a hint of a British accent as he placed her bag in front of her and held out the wallet to her.

Zora felt her ears grow warm. How had he known she was the owner of the wallet? Could he have seen the thief take it? Could he have stopped the pickpocket somehow?

The man stood in front of her and waited for her response.

"Thank you," she said as she accepted the wallet. He seemed to be about her age, handsome in a rugged way, though his close-cropped dark hair made him look younger. But something about his piercing blue eyes—clear like the crystal sky, yet neither warm nor cold—drew her in. It was like she recognized him at some level as a kindred spirit, which was weird since she'd never met him before.

"Have a good day, ma'am," he said as he adjusted the backpack strap on his shoulder, turned, and walked away, the tails of his coat flapping behind him.

Zora watched him leave. Though something about him intrigued her, Zora ignored it and said nothing as he made his way through the arrival terminal until he exited through the nearest sliding doors. She'd become wary of strangers after all she'd been through—kidnappings, brushes with serial killers, arrests, time in detention, and other near-death experiences. When all she'd ever wanted was to live a quiet life helping patients. And though the man had rescued her wallet, the part of her that had lived through more than one conspiracy wondered if he'd set the whole thing up so she would notice him. But to what aim?

Yet even if he seemed like one of the good guys, every man she'd ever been entangled with had sacrificed for her in one way or the other. First it had been Marcus, her wonderful friend and big brother, murdered while helping her, and then Dave, her now ex-boyfriend, who'd gone into the witness protection program to stop the attacks on Zora and her family. Zora wanted none of that sacrifice again.

Never again, she'd promised herself.

Zora had put that life behind her. All she wanted now was to focus on the colorectal fellowship she'd bagged, despite all her difficulties at Lexinbridge Regional Hospital where she'd done her residency. It was back to work on Monday, and Zora needed to get home and spend one more night with her family at her mom's estate before moving back to her apartment and prepping for the busy days ahead. Maybe she'd even get to hang out with her roommate, Christina, before life became too hectic.

Christina had been her best friend since high school and was also a nurse at Lexinbridge Regional. Though they were housemates, Zora had seen less of her since she'd gotten engaged to Brian Atkinson, a fellow general surgeon and Zora's buddy. Brian had also gotten a trauma fellowship at Lexinbridge Regional, and Zora was looking forward to working with him again in the ER, which she expected to be as busy as ever.

So she had no room in her life for new guys. Her only goals were to work on her research ideas, complete her fellowship, treat patients, and hang out with her friends and family. Yes, that was all she was going to allow in her life. Everything else—including the blue-eyed stranger she'd just met—was best forgotten.

Zora tucked her wallet back into her jacket, grabbed her hand luggage, and headed out of the terminal to catch the bus that would take her to airport parking.

She'd vowed to forget about the past and start anew.

Nothing and no one was going to stand in her way of enjoying her life as she saw fit.

The mid-morning sun burned hot on Zora's skin as she unlocked her car, dropped her hand luggage in the backseat, and slipped into the driver's seat. She never knew what weather to expect this early in September in Lexinbridge, but it seemed summer wasn't quite ready to let go here, unlike the cool temperatures she'd experienced in Europe. But Zora kept her fall jacket on, since she knew it could change any moment.

She drove out of the lot, exited the airport thoroughfare, and got on the state highway that led back into Lexinbridge city. Soon she arrived at the toll booth on the turnpike and waited in line to be attended to. Though there were only two cars ahead of hers, it seemed the driver at the head of the line didn't have ready cash, which meant she was in for quite a wait. *He must be a stranger to these parts*, Zora thought. Anyone who lived in Lexinbridge knew better than to approach the toll booth without cash in hand.

Zora retrieved her wallet from her jacket and set it on the passenger seat. Then she pulled out her phone and dialed Christina's number while she waited.

"Zora, you just woke me up from the most delicious dream!" Christina protested, her voice loud and clear over the car's speakers.

Zora chuckled and placed her phone in one of the car's cup holders. "Hello to you too." From experience, it was best not to ask Christina what the dream had been all about—she never remembered. "You realize it's about eleven a.m., right?"

"It's Saturday, for goodness' sake. I'm allowed to be lazy."

"I thought Brian would be at the apartment by now. You guys are practically joined at the hip."

Christina sighed. "I wish. He left for Boston this morning to see his parents."

"When is he coming back?"

"Tomorrow night." Christina yawned. "Are you still at the airport?"

"At the tollbooth. I'm waiting to pay the fare." By now, the attendant was handing over some change to the driver in the car ahead of hers, which meant it would be Zora's turn soon. She wasn't sure how the first driver had resolved his issue so fast. "I have to go. I'll see you soon."

"Great. I have some news for you too. Grab some donuts for me from that bakery on Main Street, will you?"

"I'll try. Bye." Zora ended the call and moved her car forward. A few minutes later, she'd paid her toll and was back on the highway.

Not three minutes from the booth, the wail of a siren filled the air.

Zora glanced at her rearview mirror only to see a state patrol car barreling its way down the highway. She hoped it wasn't gunning for her, since Zora did her best to stay within the speed limit, no matter what road she was on. She slowed down and entered the lane on her left to make way for the patrol car. But to Zora's surprise, the patrol car with the flashing emergency lights swerved into the lane right behind her.

Oh shoot! It really was for her. Her heart pounding, Zora decelerated, pulled over to the shoulder of the highway, and came to a stop. The state police car followed suit and parked behind her. Her heart rate spiked as she turned off her engine, rolled down her window, and placed her hands on the steering wheel. Zora watched the cop exit his vehicle and then make his way to her side of the car with trepidation—her history with the police had made her wary of them. The recent stories she'd also heard of police brutality weren't helping either.

The cop reached her door. "License and registration, please," he said.

Zora reached for her wallet on the passenger seat and pulled out her driver's license. Then she opened her glove compartment, retrieved a folded sheet of paper, and handed both items over to the cop.

He called up her license number on his radio as his eyes darted around her car and back to her. While she waited, Zora noted his badge number and committed it to memory.

The cop listened to the feedback on the radio and then handed the items back to her. Zora placed them on the front passenger seat. Hopefully, this was the end of whatever this check was supposed to be.

But he kept his eyes leveled at her. "Ma'am, what do you have in your trunk?" he asked.

Zora hid her surprise. What did that have to do with anything, and why did he want to know? Zora had nothing of significance there, but she didn't trust the police one bit.

"Ma'am, I need you to open your trunk," the cop insisted.

A feeling of unease snaked up the back of Zora's neck. This was nuts. What did he think she had there? It was just her luck to end up with one of the crazies today. Did he think she didn't know he could plant something there if she wasn't watchful? But Zora knew her rights, no matter what his intentions were. "I do not consent to a search," she said.

"Ma'am, please step out of the vehicle," the cop said.

Zora's heart pounded so loudly she was sure the cop could hear it. But she forced herself to take a deep breath. "Officer, what seems to be the problem?" Zora asked. She'd done nothing wrong to deserve this.

"Ma'am, please step out of the car," he repeated. She could see his body tense.

Crap. Zora didn't need anyone shooting her for asking a reasonable question, so she opened the door, got out of the car, and shut the door behind her. She noticed another patrol car had pulled up. A second cop with sandy brown hair stepped out and strode over to the first cop, who said something to him that Zora couldn't overhear. From the way they talked, it appeared the second cop was a superior of some sorts.

The sandy-haired cop gave her a quick glance and headed to the trunk. Zora watched him study something, but she couldn't see what it was from where she stood. What was it about her trunk that was so fascinating?

The second cop straightened and then headed to her door and jerked it open.

How dare he open her car! Mad fury bubbled up within her, but Zora tamped it down. She needed to stay in control. "I don't consent to a search," she repeated.

The sandy-haired cop ignored her, pulled the trunk lever near the brakes, and her trunk popped open.

An overpowering rusty smell hit her nostrils, and Zora almost retched.

As a doctor and a surgeon, she could recognize that scent anywhere. How had it ended up in her trunk?

Zora became lightheaded, and her vision narrowed. *Get it together, Zora,* she thought to herself. This was not the time for a panic attack, not when her life had turned into a horror movie.

She forced herself to maintain a calm façade even as she felt the full brunt of the first cop's eyes on her. Something was going on, though she didn't know what, and Zora needed to hold herself together long enough to figure it out.

The second cop rounded the side of her car and stilled for a second as he looked into the open trunk.

Zora's heart galloped. What was in her trunk? A

dead animal? A dead body? No, it couldn't be. There'd been nothing in it when she'd parked her car at the airport and gone on her trip. If this was a prank, it wasn't funny.

The second officer gave a quick nod to the first cop, who then turned to Zora. "Ma'am, you're under arrest on the charge of second-degree murder. Put your hands behind your back."

Zora's heart sank like a rock thrown into the river. It was a dead body. She'd only just arrived back in town, and her life was already turning into a mess. How had the body gotten into her car?

But she still had the presence of mind to say, "I want a lawyer," even as she complied. She winced when a set of handcuffs clamped over her wrists.

At that moment, Zora wished she'd never returned to Lexinbridge. She would have stayed in Europe if it meant not returning to this nightmare. As they guided her into the back of the patrol car, she fought to remain calm while she felt her hopes and dreams for a quiet life crash and burn to the ground.

Then Zora set her lips in a grim line. She deserved her peaceful life, for goodness' sake! Her life was hers to live as she saw fit, and she was no longer the naïve medical student and surgical resident.

It was time to put an end to all this nonsense with cops and murderers.

Zora planned to fight for her life, and winning was her only option.

Not even a dead body was going to take that away from her.

Zora rubbed her wrists as she stepped out through the doors of the police building with Silas Park at her side. Silas, besides being a well-known criminal lawyer in the city, was both her mom's boyfriend and a partner at her law firm. He was family and had come to Zora's aid every time she'd run into trouble with the law.

"Are you okay?" Silas asked, his eyes searching hers in concern.

Zora gave him a small smile. "I'm fine," she said. "Just a little shaken."

Though the building she'd just exited differed from the police station she was used to, it still gave Zora the creeps. She wasn't sure if she'd ever get over the feeling. How Zora had stayed sane throughout the ordeal she'd just gone through was still a mystery.

"I'm sorry I interrupted your afternoon schedule," she said to him. Zora had seen very little of Silas in recent weeks—her mom had stated he'd been busy with a high-profile case.

Silas waved her apology away. "I'm just glad we could get you out."

They'd released Zora from custody once it'd been confirmed she'd been out of the country and in the air at the body's estimated time of death, though she remained a suspect, according to the detectives. They'd held her car as evidence for further investigation, but had released her luggage, and Silas now held it in his hand.

She'd also been in a hurry to leave the interrogation room, that she hadn't bothered to inquire if they'd identified the body.

But now Zora wanted to know.

"Did they say who the victim was?" she asked Silas.

Silas shook his head. "They're being tight-lipped about it. I honestly think they don't have that information yet. But I assume they will soon."

Zora nodded. Maybe the victim's identity would shed more light on this new problem. But no matter how much she wanted to figure out what was going on right now and who had thrown her into this mess, she was jet lagged, exhausted, and needed rest before anything else.

She turned to Silas. "Let's go to Mom's place," she said.

Zora's mom, Adrianna Smyth, hugged Zora as soon as she stepped through the front door and into the foyer of her large home. Her late father's watercolor paintings—one of her favorite things in the world—lined the hallway, but Zora barely noticed them now.

She'd grown up here before moving into her own apartment for college, hardly came home after that because of her then broken relationship with her mom, but returned after her missing younger sister had finally come home. Zora had only moved back to her apartment once she'd started fellowship a month ago. However, experience had taught her to stay close to her family home whenever she faced major trouble, so here she was.

"Oh my goodness, Zora. Are you alright?" her mom asked, her warm eyes filled with concern.

Zora returned her hug. "I'm fine, Mom," she said,

though she felt far from it. But she couldn't allow her mom to worry. Adrianna Smyth, owner of one of the biggest law firms in the city, was a master at maintaining a calm demeanor under stress. However, given how much trouble Zora had gotten into in recent times, she worried her mom might break one of these days.

Her mom released Zora and turned to Silas. "Thanks," she said.

"Always a pleasure," he replied, and gave her mom's hand a squeeze.

Zora strode into the living room with her mom and Silas at her heels. She was bone-tired even though it was only afternoon, and all she wanted to do was scrub the stink of the police station off her skin and take a nap. "I'm going up," she said, collecting her carry-on bag from Silas.

"Okay," her mom responded without protest, though she was probably dying to know the details of what had happened. But Zora was sure Silas would bring her up to speed.

Zora bypassed the large coffee table where her mom had placed a tray with snacks and drinks—she wasn't hungry—and trudged up the winding staircase that led to the upstairs bedrooms. She soon entered her room, dropped her bag on the floor, removed the jacket she'd kept on throughout her ordeal at the station, and collapsed on her bed. Zora turned to her side as she inhaled the crisp smell of freshly laundered linen. She would have to change the beddings again after her shower, but she didn't mind. Zora just needed to relax first.

The scent reminded her of new beginnings.

Just like she'd wanted her life to have, yet it seemed she could never get rid of the stench of murders, crimes, and other terrible things from her life. What was it about her that got her entangled in these kinds of messes?

Zora sat up. She couldn't allow this to continue. Once she'd eradicated this current problem from her life, she had to make them stop once and for all, though she wasn't yet sure how. Zora just knew she was going to make it happen. This was her life, and she had every right to pursue whatever she wanted. Besides, it wasn't something unattainable she desired —lots of people had drama-free lives, and Zora deserved the same.

A knock sounded on her door, and Zora looked up to see her younger sister, Alisa, step in as the door swung open. "Hey," Alisa said.

Zora gave her a small smile and patted the space beside her. Alisa sat down. Some days, it was still hard to believe that Alisa was back in her life. But seeing the younger version of her mom, with the same honey-colored hair and high cheekbones, reassured her it was all very real. Though Dave's sacrifice and departure from Zora's life had come between them, since Alisa had unwittingly played a part in it, Zora had already forgiven her, and Alisa had spent the last few weeks trying to make it up to her.

"How are you feeling?" Alisa asked, her eyes searching Zora's face.

Zora ran a hand over her hair. "Like crap. But I'm sure I'll be better after a shower and a nap. What about Sparky?" Sparky was Alisa's one-eyed chihuahua and an absolute darling. He'd charmed everyone in the house, and they were all besotted with him.

"I took him to the vet for his usual shots today, so he's taking a nap now," Alisa replied. She touched Zora's arm. "I just wanted to pop by and check on you." Then she wrinkled her nose. "But I gotta say: you stink."

Zora grabbed her into a bear hug. "Really? I'm going to share it with you. Sharing is caring after all," she said with a wicked grin.

Alisa pushed her off. "Ugh. Now I have to go take a shower again!"

Zora pulled her into another hug, this one much softer. "I'm okay."

Alisa let out a sigh. "I was worried," she said quietly.

"I know. Sorry."

Alisa straightened, and her eyes found Zora's. "You don't have to be. You did nothing wrong."

Zora released her. "Do you think it was a coincidence?" Alisa had an uncanny sense for these types of things, given a mobster had raised her after her kidnap.

"I want to say yes, but I'm not sure," Alisa replied.

"Do you think it will get worse?"

"It might. Or not." Then Alisa gave her a determined look. "But no matter what, we'll get through it together as a family."

Yes, they would. They'd done it before and would do it again. Zora laid her head on her sister's shoulder.

Alisa rubbed her back, and Zora soon felt her worries ease away.

She would never give up fighting for the life she deserved, no matter who the enemy was.

And it would be all worth it as long as she had her family and friends by her side.

4

The woman's face displayed no emotions as she listened to the person on the other end of the line. Then she dropped the phone back in its cradle.

Idiots. She'd been a fool to trust them to get the job done right. No matter how efficient they'd been in the past, they'd botched her simple order when it mattered most. Still, she was sure the cops couldn't trace the kill back to her.

She never suffered fools, so she debated how to punish the goons for their mistake. In this business, discipline was important. There was no other way to make sure no one took you for granted. As her mind raced through methods of punishment, she picked up the little knife with the decorative bone handle from the top of her desk and twirled it like she'd always done.

The knife didn't look like much, but that was what she loved most about it—it was small, unassuming, yet lethal. She kept its edge sharp, and even though the wrong flick of her wrist could cause a nasty cut, it didn't stop her from playing with it and relishing the excitement of flirting with danger, of experiencing the rush from unforeseen surprises and unpredicted pleasures.

Then she remembered what else the person had said on the call, and she smiled.

What she'd heard had been unexpected, making her plan turn out much better than she'd hoped for. Who would have thought the doctor would get roped in and arrested instead? It wasn't what she'd arranged, but it fit right in with what she'd wanted. In fact, it made it better.

She jabbed the knife into an apple sitting on a small plate on her desk, lifted it, and took a big bite.

The punishment for the goons would wait for now, since their mistake had earned these unexpected results.

Now all she had to do was watch, wait, and take action when needed.

She took another bite of the apple and chewed.

Yes, her plan was coming along just fine.

5

Zora struggled to breathe. Strong hands gripped her throat like a vise.

She beat, scratched, and pushed against the assailant's hands to tear them away from her neck, but to no avail.

Her eyes swung wildly around her, searching for something, anything she could use, but there was nothing she could grasp on the concrete floor her attacker pressed her against. The vertical iron bars surrounding the space reminded her of the prison cell she'd been in many months ago. Yet nobody came to her rescue, no matter how much she tried to scream for help.

No! She couldn't give in. No one had the right to take her life away.

Her heart swelled with anger, and the rage of all the injustices she'd ever suffered welled up inside her like stormy waters. With a strength she didn't know she had, Zora clawed at the assailant's face.

He cried out as he released his grip and groped for his eyes.

Zora sprang up, her lungs gulping in air like it was running out of supply. Her first instinct was to run toward the bars and try to get out, but she had a feeling this monster would come after her again and again if she didn't stand her ground.

Zora turned back and faced him, her fists clenched tight at her sides.

He snarled, and in that moment, though she couldn't see his face, her heart recognized him as the enemy who'd cornered her on every side and had now tried to kill her.

A wave of hatred against him rose within her, and with a fierce cry, she sprang into the air…

Zora jerked awake, her sweat-soaked hair plastered around her face, and her chest heaving.

She took deep breaths as she tried to slow her racing heart. Then she swept the hair away from her face.

It had only been a dream. Another nightmare.

Zora checked the alarm clock on her nightstand.

It was eleven thirty-five p.m.—she'd only slept for a few hours after forgoing dinner.

She got up, washed her face, and changed out of her sweat-soaked pajamas into a nightshirt and shorts. Then Zora climbed back into bed, her knees drawn up against her chest, and rested her back against the headboard as she tried to make sense of what had just happened.

Why another nightmare now? Was it because of today's arrest? Zora wanted to believe so, but she couldn't forget her nightmares tended to be warnings of what was to come. Did the dream mean her life was going to be in danger soon? Was it related to the body they'd found in her trunk?

She sighed. Zora didn't know what to think. Yet this nightmare appeared different. For the first time, she'd fought back on the offensive. Even though Zora had started off as a victim, she'd turned on her assailant. Did it mean whatever was coming would play out differently this time around? Or would she lose herself?

Zora ran a hand through her hair. Well, she was Dr. Zora Smyth, a survivor of all things terrible. She wasn't going to lose, no matter what events came her way. Zora had pulled through before, and she could do so again.

She stretched out on the bed and lay on her side. For now, she would do her best to avoid any kind of trouble. But if danger came anyway, she would fight with everything, like she had in the dream, to overcome it. Her life was worth that much. If she didn't already know, Marcus and Dave had proven it clearly.

Zora remained that way as the minutes ticked by, her hands tucked under her head.

Then sleep overcame her.

Zora stepped into her apartment the next morning and engaged the deadbolt behind her. Despite her mom's urgings to stay, she'd chosen to come back to her place. This was where she felt most comfortable when she had to deal with work, and Zora had to show up at the hospital come Monday.

She dropped her carry-on luggage in the closet by the door, removed her shoes, and made her way past the pale mint and grey kitchen into the living room. The place was quieter than she'd expected—maybe Christina was not home.

Her eyes scanned the area. Zora loved this space she called her own. This right here was her special place, though she enjoyed staying with her mom and sister at the house where she'd grown up.

Sure, it was the same apartment from which she'd been kidnapped and arrested, and someone had even vandalized the place a few months ago. Yet it was here she'd had the best times with Christina throughout those years of college, medical school, and residency, and where she'd dealt with cancer until she'd gone into remission. She'd even met Dave here for the first time since they'd broken up in high school and had fallen in love with him all over again.

A dull ache filled her chest at her memories of him, and Zora rubbed at it as if to make the pain go away. She still missed him something fierce, though not as bad as before. Zora still found it hard to believe she'd never see him again. But everything that had happened was in the past, and she couldn't change it. All she could do now was take one step at a time and move forward with her life.

She flopped on the color-splattered couch and placed her feet on the coffee table. The mint green and silver polka dot curtains were closed, yet Zora could see the faint rays of the late-morning sun peeking through. She turned her head over her shoulder and glanced at her green plants in the room's corner. They still looked good, even if she'd forgotten to water them in her hurry to catch her flight. Christina must have taken care of them—she knew how much the plants meant to Zora.

"Hey, you're back!" a familiar voice said.

Zora looked up to see the gorgeous redhead standing by the door to her room in her pajamas, her glorious hair looking like a windstorm had blown through it. "I didn't know you were in," Zora said.

Christina yawned as she sauntered over to the couch, dropped beside Zora, and wrapped her in a hug. "I'm so glad you're okay. It took everything in me not to rush over to your mom's house."

Zora gave her a small smile. "I'm glad you held back the urge. I needed to be alone."

Christina straightened, and her eyes scanned Zora's. "How are you doing?"

Zora shrugged. "I'm hanging in there."

Christina gave her another squeeze. "You'll be fine. Eventually."

"Thanks for watering the plants."

"You're welcome." Then Christina released her. "Were you able to find out what happened?"

Zora shook her head. "Not yet. But Silas is looking into it."

Christina leaned back. "But why would someone dump a body in your car of all vehicles?"

"I know, right?"

"Something tells me it's not a coincidence."

"I'm hoping it is," Zora said. "Because you know what? I've had enough of this kind of drama."

"I'm sure. Have they identified the body?"

"Silas said they're still working on it."

"I'm just glad they could confirm your alibi."

"Me too." Zora shuddered. "I can't even imagine going back in there." Zora didn't need to specify where for Christina to understand what she'd meant. Zora had been to jail once and had no desire to return there. She'd fight tooth and nail before she'd let that happen.

Christina squeezed Zora's arm. "Have you eaten?" she asked.

Zora leaned against her. "Not yet. I figured I'd have breakfast with you."

"Awesome. Toast and eggs coming right up," Christina said with a smile.

Fifteen minutes later, Christina placed a plate of toast, scrambled eggs, and sausage in front of Zora. "Here you go," she said.

Zora flashed her a smile. "Thank you." She was now seated on one of the bar stools at the kitchen counter with a cup of her favorite Yergacheffe coffee in hand.

"You're welcome." Christina grabbed her own plate and sat on another bar stool. Then they ate in silence.

"So, what's the news you mentioned on the phone yesterday?" Zora asked Christina after a few minutes.

Christina dropped her fork on the plate and faced Zora. "I'm starting a new rotation tomorrow."

"A new shift?"

Christina shook her head. "I'll be working in interventional radiology for the next two months."

Zora's eyebrows rose, and she took a sip of her coffee. "Radiology? How did that happen?"

"I've been thinking about becoming a nurse practitioner—"

"Finally!"

Christina chuckled. "I knew you'd say that. I don't know why I held back all this time."

"Exactly." Zora set her mug on the countertop. "I wouldn't have nagged you so much about it if it wasn't something you've always said you wanted. But I'm glad you've taken the step." She pinched Christina's cheeks.

Christina swatted Zora's hands away. "Oh, knock it off."

Zora chuckled. "You know you like it." She propped her chin on her palm. "I'm happy for you.

But what does radiology have to do with becoming an NP? I thought you'd be interested in Trauma or Surgical." Christina had trained both as a trauma nurse and an OR nurse and had extensive experience in both.

"Well, I figured I'd scratch it off my bucket list before I focus on the NP. You know, the whole 'no regrets' thing. Radiology is an area I've always been curious about. Besides, interventional radiology is still relevant to surgical nursing. The nursing director owed me a favor, so now I've got two months to try it out."

"Just make sure you're careful. You and Brian are getting married soon, and you know what they say about radiation and buns in the oven." Christina smacked Zora's arm. "Ouch! What was that for?"

Christina chuckled. "Keep your mind out of the gutter. You know I'll take all the safety precautions." Then her face turned serious. "Marriage is another reason I want to do it now. Brian and I are on the same page about me doing whatever I want in the future, yet I feel like I'll be too busy after marriage to want to experiment."

Zora pulled her into a hug. "I'm happy for you, my friend. Even though I'll miss your face in the ER."

Christina returned the hug. "I'm happy for me, too. But…"

Zora pulled back and scanned her face. "But what?"

Christina ran a hand through her hair. "I don't know. I'm excited about radiology and all, yet I can't help having this uneasy feeling whenever I think about it."

"Why?"

"I don't know. I've met the folks there, and they're nice, but something keeps nagging me at the back of my mind about it. It feels like… something terrible is going to happen."

Zora could have brushed Christina's concerns away, but experience had taught her to pay attention to her instincts. She would expect Christina to do the same. "Do you want to turn the rotation down?"

"No. I mean, I still want to do it. I'm just wondering if the feeling is a sign, you know."

Well, it seemed all Christina wanted was some reassurance that everything would be alright. Zora placed her hands on Christina's arms. "I'm sure it'll be fine."

Christina exhaled. "Okay. If you say so. I'm excited about it, though."

Zora tweaked her nose. "That's my girl."

Christina gave her a mock stern look. "Zora dearest, if you tweak my nose again, I'll kick your behind."

Zora laughed and turned back to her food. "Let's finish before the eggs get cold." She smiled as Christina dove back into her meal.

But Zora hoped everything would be alright. It was already bad enough she had to deal with the latest setback in her life. The last thing Zora needed was for Christina's life to turn upside down as well. Both their work lives had to remain the stable anchors they needed.

And speaking of the workplace, Zora hoped the news about her arrest hadn't reached the hospital.

6

Zora let out a sigh of relief as she strode into the ER on Monday evening. So far, no one had mentioned anything about her arrest, nor had she gotten any weird looks throughout the day—it seemed the hospital's rumor mill hadn't received the news, which was what she'd hoped for. Zora hadn't been so lucky with the ill-reputed grapevine in the past.

"What do we have here?" she asked Elias Duncan, the senior surgical resident-on-call, as she arrived by the side of the patient they'd paged her for. The patient was in one of the ER's cubicles.

"Toby Fisher, a forty-two-year-old male, diagnosed with Stage I colorectal cancer two weeks ago at our clinic—"

"Under which surgeon?"

"Dr. Clark," the resident said as he pushed his black-rimmed glasses up his nose.

Perfect, Zora thought. Since Dr. Clark was the attending-on-call for the day, and that would make managing the patient easier.

"Continue," she said as she donned the pair of gloves she'd grabbed from a dispenser near the nursing station.

Elias adjusted his glasses. "He presented at the ER fifteen minutes ago, complaining of sudden abdominal pain that started this morning. No history of abdominal trauma, dialysis, or ascites. No change in urine output. Patient is conscious but in moderate distress with a Glasgow coma scale of fourteen—Mr. Fisher can only hold confused conversations, though he's able to answer questions. No other neurological deficits are present.

"He has a fever of one hundred and one degrees Fahrenheit, a respiratory rate of twenty-four breaths per minute, and a heart rate of one hundred and four beats per minute. Lungs are clear and well perfused, BP is one-twenty over eighty-five, and the heart is in sinus rhythm with no obvious cardiac abnormalities.

"There's localized guarding and tenderness in the left lumbar region, and bowel sounds are absent.

We've sent blood for a full workup—we're expecting the results soon. The ER doctor prescribed some IV fluids, painkillers, and antibiotics for him in the meantime. Patient is sleeping now."

"Any rectal bleeding?"

"Minimal."

"Any vomiting?"

"None."

"What about the lymph nodes?" Zora asked.

"No notable enlargements," Elias said.

"CT scan?"

"Done. Awaiting results."

Zora turned to the ER nurse, who she'd noticed at the cubicle's entrance. Zora had worked with Nora multiple times in the past. "Can we get someone to track down the results of the CT scan?"

"I'll call radiology," the brunette replied.

"Thanks."

Nora left the cubicle, and Zora focused back on the patient, who she'd woken. Then she examined him to confirm what the resident had shared. The patient fell back asleep as soon as she was done.

"So, what's your preliminary diagnosis?" Zora asked as she discarded the gloves she'd used and donned another set.

Elias pushed up his glasses before replying.

"Bowel perforation secondary to colorectal cancer. Patient has a history of cancer from previous results."

Zora had come to the same conclusion, but she needed imaging diagnostic results to confirm it if she was going to send the patient into surgery. If the working diagnosis was right, then it was concerning that the patient had progressed from Stage 1 to Stage 2B so quickly—it could even be worse than that. Since the CT scan was delayed—from a busy Monday schedule and an unusually packed ER— Zora couldn't wait for it. Time was of the essence for this patient before his condition deteriorated to a life-threatening stage, which could happen any moment. "Let's get the ultrasound cart."

"Already here." Nora had returned with the portable trolley ultrasound system. It was as if she'd read Zora's mind.

Zora gave her a warm smile. "Thank you."

The corners of Nora's lips turned up. "Any time."

Zora kicked a nearby stool closer, sat down, and prepped the patient for the ultrasound. "What kind of perforation do you think we have here, Dr. Duncan?" she asked the resident.

Elias didn't even hesitate. "Most likely at the tumor site."

Zora looked up at him. "Why do you think so?"

"I'd have expected the symptoms to be more severe if it were proximal to the tumor site," Elias replied. "The abdominal guarding and tenderness would have been more generalized as well."

"Are you sure?"

Elias hesitated for a moment. "Yes," he then said.

"Okay. Let's see what Mr. Fisher's body tells us."

Zora began the abdominal ultrasound. As she expected in perforation cases, she found gas shadowing along the peritoneum with free gas limited to the pelvis. Thankfully, there was no obvious obstruction. The ultrasound's findings were enough to schedule an emergency surgery for the patient to address the perforation before it worsened, though she hoped the CT scan would be available by then for better isolation of the problem areas.

A loud blare from the cardiac monitor rent the air.

Zora's eyes snapped to the monitor. The patient's blood pressure was crashing!

Crap! Now she needed to stabilize the patient before they could head into surgery. She turned to Nora. "I need one milligram of epinephrine IV and two liters of saline with IV crystalloid going in at maximum flow rate right now."

"On it," Nora replied, and hurried out of the cubicle.

"Let's check for any rectal bleeding," Zora ordered.

Elias obeyed. "Patient is bleeding a little more than before, but it's not significant enough to be causing this drop in blood pressure," he said.

So if it wasn't from the bleeding, then this patient could end up with peritonitis, which could be fatal if not addressed immediately. The patient's condition had deteriorated faster than she'd expected.

Zora checked his Glasgow coma scale status. Mr. Fisher now scored a thirteen on the scale, which meant a drop in his level of consciousness but not enough to be in the trouble zone yet. The patient was still breathing on his own, and his lungs were clear, yet it was better to be safe than sorry. "Let's get some oxygen on him," she said. Zora had also reviewed his drug chart on her way in, and the antibiotics already prescribed were within the limits needed by the patient, so she didn't have to make any adjustments there.

Elias placed an oxygen mask over the patient's face, and Nora returned with the crash cart and another nurse in tow. The second nurse adjusted the fluids to Zora's specifications, while Nora injected the epinephrine into the IV line.

Zora's eyes scanned the cardiac monitor. Its

wailing sound continued to fill the air, though the patient's heart remained in sinus rhythm. The BP was still dropping, but at a slower rate.

Tension filled the air like a balloon waiting to pop.

Come on, come on, Zora thought as she willed the BP descent to reverse. As much as she itched to do something, she had to give the drugs time to work their magic. Her eyes stayed fixed on the cardiac monitor, though she remained alert, ready to intervene further if the patient's body didn't respond as expected.

Then the BP climbed, and the blare stopped.

A deafening silence filled the air, but then the monitor returned to its typical rhythmic beeping.

Zora could feel the room's collective sigh of relief. Still, they were not out of the woods yet.

"Let's get this patient into the OR and page Dr. Clark about him."

"I'll page Dr. Clark and get the transfer going," Nora promised.

"Thank you," Zora replied. Nora left with the second nurse.

Zora turned to Elias. "We need the CT scan and blood work reports ASAP, even if you have to go there and get them yourself."

"On it," Elias said, already hurrying out of the ER cubicle.

Zora's eyes stayed on the patient, and she continued to observe him—she'd remain until Elias or a nurse returned.

A noise behind her made her turn. Sally Grange, the resident on call in the inpatient colorectal unit, had just entered the room.

"Dr. Smyth," Sally said.

"What is it, Dr. Grange?" Zora asked. "Are the patients okay?" Zora had done a quick round with Sally a few hours ago, and the patients had been stable at the time. But that could always change in the blink of an eye.

"Um… I…"

Zora's eyes searched Sally's face. This was unlike her—the dark-skinned resident was confident, smart, great under pressure, and Zora had always enjoyed working with her. Zora's curiosity piqued at what might have been causing her discomfort. "You can tell me. It's fine," Zora reassured her.

Sally pulled out a tablet from behind her and showed Zora the screen.

Zora accepted it and scanned the patient care order on it. It was for Henry Frost, a diverticulitis patient who'd they'd admitted last week and had now developed a fistula. He was scheduled for surgery in two days. "What should I be looking at?"

"I just wondered about the diagnostic tests that were ordered," Sally said.

Zora studied the ordered tests. They included an abdominal ultrasound and an MRI. She looked up in surprise. "I thought the patient already had a CT scan done a few hours ago. These requests weren't there during our earlier rounds." The patient didn't need these additional tests, since the CT scan results would be out before the day of surgery.

Sally nodded. "Yes, to both statements. That's why I figured I should bring it to your attention."

Zora noted the name of the attending who'd ordered the tests: Dr. Clark. It was a good thing she'd be seeing him in the operating room shortly. She'd ask him about it after the surgery. But Sally had been brave to bring it to her notice. It could have backfired if not handled delicately.

"I'll take care of it," Zora said to Sally.

Sally's shoulders relaxed. "Thank you. Will you be back for another round later tonight?"

"Hmmm… maybe after my emergency surgery. But you don't have to wait for me. I'll page you if I need you."

"Thank you, Dr. Smyth." Then Sally turned and left.

Zora mulled the situation over in her mind. Why would Dr. Clark have ordered the tests? The whole thing seemed excessive.

The more she thought about it, the more she became troubled. But Zora shrugged away her concerns. Maybe it had only been a mistake and not such a big deal as her mind was making it out to be. All she had to do was bring it up with Dr. Clark.

But something warned her the situation might not be as simple as it appeared.

7

Zora cranked her neck from side to side as she scrubbed her hands in the semi-restricted area of the operating room suite. The emergency surgery had taken longer than expected, but they'd taken out as much tumor as possible from Mr. Fisher's intestines and close off the perforation. Fortunately, the patient hadn't needed a colostomy, and Zora hoped he'd make a quick recovery.

She heard the shuffling of feet and looked up to see Dr. Clark enter the room. He filled the space with his tall frame and wide shoulders. Sporting a blond crew cut, Dr. Clark could have been mistaken for an ex-marine. Zora had been waiting for him, since he'd hung back for a few minutes to chat with the anesthe-siologist.

Dr. Clark headed to another sink, and soon only the sound of running water reigned in the air as they scrubbed their hands in silence.

Once she'd dried hers, Zora turned to Dr. Clark. There was no one else around. "Dr. Clark, I have a question for you regarding Henry Frost," she said.

Zora thought she saw him stiffen for a moment and then relax. "Henry Frost?"

"Yes. The diverticulitis patient that we recently admitted."

He dried his hands. "Oh. What about him?"

"I noticed you ordered both an abdominal ultrasound and an MRI for him."

"Yes, I did. Is that a problem?"

"He's already had a CT scan done, and the results should be available soon."

"The patient needs those tests for better evaluation of his condition. For the surgery."

"But—"

Dr. Clark stepped closer to her, and Zora fought the urge to step back. "Dr. Smyth, is it?"

"Yes."

His eyes grew cold. "I've heard all about you and how you look for trouble where it doesn't exist.

Given your reputation, I would be careful if I were you. There's only so far your skills will take you if you don't learn to mind your business. Or are you trying to usurp my authority as the attending?"

Zora kept her chin up and maintained eye contact with him. Contrary to what he seemed to think, she didn't like trouble. But she hated being bullied more. "Not at all," she said in an even tone. "We all want what's best for this patient, and I'm just trying to understand the rationale for your treatment protocol."

"The patient needs it, got it? That's all there is to it."

"If you say so, Dr. Clark."

He studied her for another moment and then brushed past her and out of the OR.

Zora turned and watched him leave. What had gotten him all twisted up? It had only been a simple question. Then why did it seem like he was hiding something?

She wasn't sure what to make of it, but maybe it was best Zora minded her business, since she couldn't override Dr. Clark's decision. The tests were also not harming the patient's health, and right now, Zora needed to avoid any unnecessary conflicts if she wanted her fellowship to go smoothly. She had to pick her battles, and this wasn't one she needed to fight.

Zora sighed and headed out after him. She needed to grab something to eat before making her way to the colorectal unit.

Maybe she'd also use the opportunity to catch up with Christina and find out how her day had gone.

———————

Zora's shoulders relaxed as she stretched out her feet on the couch positioned in the center of the fellows' lounge. The space was bigger than the one she'd used during residency, though it had the same configuration—large windows lining one side with workstations on all other sides. The brown curtains were open, and Zora could see the stars twinkling like faraway gems in the dark sky.

A small conference table hugged another section of the room, and Zora's research materials were laid out on it. Thankfully, she was the only one using the space, which was how it had been for most of the nights she'd been on call.

Dinner had been a formerly-hot-but-now-cold ham and cheese sandwich, and Zora had washed down the bland taste with a bottle of orange juice.

Now all she wished for was a few minutes of quiet and rest.

She shut her eyes as she forced herself to relax.

After a while, she opened them, pulled out her phone, and dialed Christina's number. The call rang twice before the line connected.

"Hey, you," Christina said, her voice sounding a little tired.

"How was your day?" Zora asked.

"Interesting. The other nurses were nice and welcoming. But we had so many patients. Who would have thought Interventional Radiology would be more tiring than the ER?"

Zora chuckled. "I'm sure that's not possible."

"That's what I thought too, before I experienced it myself."

Zora laughed. "Congrats on surviving your first day."

"Thank you very much."

Zora placed her free arm behind her head. "So, did you meet any hot doctors?"

"Need I remind you I'm taken?"

"That has never stopped your eyes from admiring God's creations."

"True." They both laughed.

"So?"

"Well, there was this one guy, Dr. Ethan Gates. Hot as could be, with dreamy blue eyes. Unfortunately, he's not my type. I prefer the ones with a little meat on them, like Brian. But Dr. Gates was very helpful today. In fact, too helpful. The other nurses joked he might have been hitting on me, but I don't believe it."

Zora turned to her side. "What if he is?"

"I'll let him know I'm not available. I might even have Brian come over one of these days and say hi if he persists. You know me. I'm a one-man kind of girl."

"That you are." Brian and Christina were so madly in love with each other that Christina wouldn't allow anyone to jeopardize what they had.

Zora's pager beeped at that moment. She pulled it from its hook on the waistband of her scrubs and checked the message. "I have to go," she said.

"Alright. Have a quiet call."

"That's my prayer. I'll talk to you later." Zora disconnected the line.

She was glad today had worked out well for Christina. Her concerns yesterday about something possibly going wrong had bothered Zora, but now it seemed she didn't have to worry anymore.

Zora rose to her feet. She had a patient waiting

that needed her. She strode over to the conference table, stashed her research materials in her bag, and donned her medical coat.

As she strode to her locker to put away her bag before heading to the ER, Zora hoped the rest of both their weeks would continue with no incident.

8

"Hello, Nurse Christina."

Christina looked up from the paperwork she'd been working on for her next patient to see Dr. Ethan Gates leaning against the radiology unit's check-in counter, which also served double duty as the nursing station. "Dr. Gates. How may I help you today?"

"Do you have a minute?"

Christina glanced around the room. Tuesday seemed to be a slower day at the unit, and though it was only ten a.m., they'd already attended to most of the morning patients. Only a few remained in the waiting room. The other nurses seemed to pay attention to their conversation, even if they feigned otherwise. But it didn't matter, since Christina had nothing private to say to him. "Go ahead."

Dr. Gates raised an eyebrow. "Here?"

"Hmmm. Is that a problem?"

"No, of course not." He lowered his voice. "I was just wondering if you'd be interested in participating in a percutaneous transhepatic cholangiography procedure. I have one scheduled for this afternoon at two p.m."

Christina perked up at his words. The other nurses may be familiar with the procedure, but Christina wasn't. She still had so much to learn in such a short time. This was an opportunity she couldn't afford to pass up. "That would be great. Thank you."

"You're welcome. I'll see you then." Dr. Gates walked away.

"That sounds like a date to me," a voice whispered beside her. Christina could tell without turning that it was Gail, a short, stocky nurse she'd befriended on her first day in the unit. The other nurses chuckled.

"It's not," Christina said.

"Keep telling yourself that," Gail replied. "Anyone can see Dr. Gates has the hots for you."

"It doesn't matter who he has the hots for. I'm not available."

"Not like that has ever stopped others before."

"I'm not others."

"I hope so, for your sake."

Christina gave her a sharp look. "What do you mean?"

Gail said nothing and continued typing on the computer in front of her.

"Tell me," Christina insisted.

"I'm sure you'll find out soon," Gail mumbled under her breath and turned back to her work.

Christina's attempts to prod her for answers halted by the buzzing of the alarm she'd set on her phone. It was time to make sure she'd prepped the intervention room for her next patient.

As she rose from her seat, one of her papers fluttered to the floor on the other side of the counter. Christina strode around the station and bent down to pick it up.

Suddenly, she felt a cold wet sensation on her back, and she sprang to her feet. A thin lady in brown scrubs was standing behind her with a mop in her hand. "I'm so sorry," she said. "I didn't see you there."

Christina wasn't sure if that was true, since she

wasn't so small as to be invisible, but she liked to give people the benefit of the doubt. Besides, her mom had raised her right, and there was no way she'd reprimand the lady in front of patients. So instead, she said nothing and looked down on her scrubs, which were now streaked with ugly brown stains. Now Christina needed a quick clean-up in addition to prepping the radiology suite, and she was running out of time.

She ignored the janitor, grabbed the sheet of paper from the floor, and rose to her feet.

"I guess you've found out why it's a bad idea," Gail murmured.

Christina's eyes widened. Did Gail mean what Christina was thinking? That this janitor was involved with Dr. Gates? She didn't care who was with who, but Dr. Gates had no business hitting on anyone if he already had someone in his life.

Now, more than ever, Christina needed to make her stand clear to him. She was only here to learn about interventional radiology and nothing else.

"Nurse Christina."

Christina turned to see Dr. Tanner, the radiologist who was in charge of her next patient.

Shoot! She hadn't expected to cross his path yet. "Yes?"

"Is everything ready?" he asked.

"Almost. I should be done soon."

He frowned as his eyes scanned her frame, noticing the brown stains. "Let's get it together, shall we?" he said.

Christina's ears turned red. *Did he have to say that?*

Then Dr. Tanner sighed, his disappointment palpable. "Let me know when you're ready."

"I will," Christina replied. This wasn't the impression she'd been hoping to make, but there was nothing she could do about it now. She just had to make sure the procedure didn't get delayed.

She collected the rest of her items from the check-in counter and hurried to the nurses' changing room.

But the barely concealed smirk on the janitor's face made Christina wonder if the whole incident had been deliberate.

Even if it was, it had only been a minor accident. It wasn't like it had turned her whole life upside down.

9

"Welcome back, Lieutenant Morris," his captain said in a gruff voice as he came around his desk and shook Morris' hand. They matched each other in their tall frames and broad builds. But where his captain had a paunch that showed a love for his wife's cooking, Morris' only standout features were his lion-mane hair and heavyset jaw.

Morris nodded, a blank expression on his face. His boss, who everyone called Captain, didn't know how glad he was to be back.

Everyone had assumed Morris had moved out of state to the New Jersey State Police for family reasons, but Morris knew the real reason. He'd botched, in his opinion, the Formalin Killer case many years ago and rather than stick around and face humiliation from his colleagues and lose his chance at a promotion, he'd taken the coward's way out.

Fortunately, his department had been testing out a new national pilot exchange program with other state police agencies, and they'd accepted Morris as one of those to represent the state. It had only been a perfect coincidence that his mother-in-law—who lived in New Jersey at the time—had needed long-term nursing care, so he'd accepted the assignment to the NJSP and had moved with his wife and kids to be with her. She'd passed on after a few years. With his program ending and his wife wanting to return to Lexinbridge, Morris had moved his family back home.

"Have a seat," Captain said as he waved him into a visitors' chair facing his desk.

Morris complied, noting the chair didn't hurt his back, like the previous ones. It seemed Captain's chairs had received an upgrade.

Captain sat behind his desk. "Did you have any problems settling back in?"

"Not at all," Morris replied. "Having yesterday off was very helpful." Morris had needed to accompany his wife to her Monday medical appointment.

"I'm glad to hear it."

"So why did you want to see me, Captain?"

"First of all, I'm glad you've taken over the lieutenant position." Morris had heard about the guy, Dave McKesson, who'd had the job before him, but not the full details on why he was no longer occupying the position. "Secondly, and more importantly, I need you to take over this fresh case we've just received, since the higher-ups agree it's in our jurisdiction. I believe this job is for you." Captain dropped a case file in front of him.

Morris accepted the file and flipped through it. What did the Captain mean? Then he turned the next page and saw it.

His heart raced. It was her.

Sure, she looked older, but he could never forget that face. It had haunted his dreams long enough for him to recognize it anywhere.

His eyes jerked up to Captain's. "What's this?"

Captain leaned back. "That's why I said I think you're the best man for the job."

Morris scanned the report. They'd found a body in her trunk. *Interesting.* Even though Alfred Pickles had confessed he was the killer in the Formalin Killer case, Morris had always found it odd that Zora Smyth had been involved. Why had the first body landed on her dissecting table when there had been so many other tables it could have been on? Why had she been there the night before? The police force had chalked it up to coincidence, but something about the case had nagged him then. He'd followed all her other cases since then, and somehow, Zora Smyth always ended up coming out of every situation smelling like roses. And now here she was again, a body in her car.

"Is she in custody?" Morris asked.

"They've released her."

"What?"

Captain twirled his handlebar mustache. "She had an iron-clad alibi. Dr. Smyth was in the air on her way into the country during the estimated time of death."

How convenient. She could very well have planned it that way—Dr. Smyth was intelligent, that was for sure. "So, what do you want me to do now?"

"We need to find the actual killer before they disappear."

Or expose Zora Smyth for the killer he was certain she was. Morris scanned the file again. "We don't know the victim?"

"Not yet, but Doc is working on it." Doc was the medical examiner at the coroner's office that handled most of their cases. "The full autopsy report should be available soon."

"Alright, I'll take the case." Not like he hadn't already decided to the moment he'd seen her photo.

"Great. I've assigned a detective to work with you. Lou Gardner, you remember him, right?"

Morris nodded. Lou had been Shepherd's boy, a rookie who'd been afraid of his own shadow when he'd joined the force. Shepherd, Morris' old partner on the Formalin Killer case—and who'd retired as the result of a medical injury—had taken Lou under his wings and worked with him until the boy had gained confidence. Morris didn't anticipate any issues working with him.

"Great. Now get out of my office."

Morris rose to his feet and headed toward the door. He couldn't wait to dig in and uncover all Zora Smyth's secrets.

"Morris," Captain called out just as he grabbed the door handle.

Morris turned back to him. "Yes, Captain."

"Just so you know. Dr. Smyth was Dave's girl-friend. For his sake, no witch hunt, got it?"

Morris stilled. He'd heard the rumors of how she'd ruined the talented detective. It was one more reason to make sure she got locked up for good. He had his plans, but he had to play it safe for now so as not to arouse Captain's suspicion. If Morris recalled correctly, it was a mistake to underestimate the Captain's intelligence—there was a reason he'd stayed at the chief's side all these years. "Got it," he said.

Captain's eyes studied Morris for a moment. Then he nodded and turned back to the paperwork that had held his attention before Morris entered his office.

Morris let himself out and shut the door behind him.

He hadn't known what to expect, but it turned out the heavens were on his side and had given him the best case he could have asked for, and a chance to redeem himself.

Morris would prove to the Captain that he'd made the right choice in placing him in charge of the case. He'd tear off Zora Smyth's fake mask of innocence and reveal her for the monster she was.

And he'd make sure nothing could save her.

The large man swung the door to the restaurant open and stepped in. Of course, he'd expected to look out of place in the swanky restaurant dressed as he was in jeans and a leather jacket, but he hadn't remembered the experience being this jarring. Yet he was used to places like this with its classy old-world interior, ornate sparkling chandeliers, and a comfortable ambience that reeked of opulence.

It was all smoke and mirrors. If he guessed correctly, there was a hidden carved staircase that led to a second level of the building, where the bigger, more profitable business stayed hidden. The one that should never be seen.

The ma"tre d, a short middle-aged man dressed in

an impeccable suit, approached him. "Good evening, sir. How may I help you?" he asked politely, though with a hint of snobbery.

The man said nothing and instead handed him a black card with gold lettering.

The ma"tre d stiffened, his shoulders bowed in submission. "This way please," he said.

He followed the ma"tre d silently as he led him along the perimeter of the restaurant and through a doorway until they reached a large door flanked by two silent armed bodyguards. The ma"tre d handed one of them the card. The bodyguard studied the card, then slipped in through the door behind him. He returned a few moments later and nodded to the ma"tre d.

The ma"tre d turned to the man. "You can go in," he said.

The man stepped through the door into a large office space. A large, monstrously ornate desk sat at its center, but the man focused instead on the handsome devil in a black silk shirt and black pants seated behind it.

"Who are you?" asked the handsome devil, Alex, in a cultured voice. Though he looked and sounded like he couldn't hurt a fly, the man was certain he was deadlier than a venomous snake—he couldn't have lasted long in the business if he wasn't.

"Wiz sent me," the man replied. Wiz, a long-time acquaintance of his, had owed him a favor, and the man had called it in.

Alex picked up a pen from his desk and played with it as he studied the man.

The man returned his gaze. He knew the pen in Alex's hands was no ordinary one, and it would be the end of him if he didn't succeed in what he'd come for. He was sure Alex had been expecting him—Wiz wouldn't have given out Alex's card unless he'd spoken to him first—and must have already run a background check on him.

Finally, Alex's face relaxed into a smile. "You'll work twenty-four hours a day, five days a week as a bodyguard, and get two days off. Does that work for you?"

"Yes, sir," the man replied. It gave him more than enough free time to take care of what had brought him back to town. He'd stayed away for a few years, traveling all over the country. But once he'd gotten some news, he'd known he had to return. Besides, his reason for leaving town was long buried, including anyone who could have traced what happened back then to him.

"Alright. Are you ready to start immediately?" Alex said.

"Yes, sir."

"Okay. See Bruno, the guard you met outside, and he'll get you all squared away."

"Okay, sir." The man turned to leave.

"So, what should we call you?" Alex asked.

The man spun back to Alex and met his gaze. "Tiny."

D r. Clark collapsed on the pristine white leather couch, one of five in the large private lounge. "Sorry I'm late," he said to the other members of the club scattered across the other pieces of luxurious furniture around him. They were in one of the many rooms in the large private mansion that they'd converted into an ultra-private club, equipped with its own golf course, tennis courts, and Olympic-sized swimming pools. No one knew who the actual owner of the mansion was, its ownership hidden under a complex layer of shell companies.

What had started off as a group of surgeon friends coming together to discuss business many decades ago had morphed into an invitation-only old boys' club of extremely wealthy surgeons in Lexinbridge. The club had become one that was only spoken of in whispers, yet most surgeons would have killed for a chance to be a part of it. But the club hardly ever admitted new members, and only those with established pedigrees at that. Even then, there was the general membership, which most members belonged to, and then the inner circle—a small, powerful cluster of surgeons at the core of the organization. The latter group were the ones here today.

"What took you so long?" Dr. Hill asked. The cynical red-haired plastic surgeon was pouring a drink for himself from the well-stocked bar that could rival any private collection.

"Just finished a brutal call. Too many emergency surgeries." Dr Clark stretched his neck from side to side. "Now I just need to unwind." He'd been a member of the club for a while but had only become part of the inner circle a few months ago.

"Here you go," Dr. Lewis said as he handed Dr. Clark a drink. The orthopedic surgeon hardly spoke unless necessary. It seemed Clark's exhaustion had merited his attention.

"Thanks," Dr. Clark said, accepting the glass and emptying it in one gulp. The liquor burned his throat, but soon warmth spread throughout his body. "I needed that."

"We should get down to business," Dr. Roberts said and nestled his tall frame in one of the high-backed leather seats. He was the unofficial head of the club and ensured it ran smoothly.

Dr. Allen, a neurosurgeon, ambled over from where he'd been reading on a tablet and plopped down beside Dr. Clark. "You can go ahead."

For the next hour, they discussed their business transactions, investments, and holdings. Even though the market had been down, they'd made a tidy sum that further strengthened the power base of their club and its influence, both at the hospital and among the movers and shakers of the city.

"Anything else?" Dr. Roberts said as they rounded up the meeting.

Dr. Clark glanced at the others before answering. "Someone's been asking questions," he said.

Dr. Hill gave him a sharp look. "Who?"

"Dr. Zora Smyth."

"I think I've heard about her," Dr. Lewis said thoughtfully. "The one who was on the news some time ago? She had that nasty business with Dr. Edwards, right?"

Dr. Clark nodded. "Yes, the same one."

"What did she want?" Dr. Roberts asked.

"She'd noticed some extra procedures I'd ordered and wanted to know why I'd requested them."

"And what did you tell her?"

"Let's just say I gave her a subtle warning to mind her business."

"We need to monitor her," Dr. Allen said. "You never know what a troublemaker like her could be up to."

"You'd think she'd have had enough of trouble with all the other issues she's had," Dr. Lewis said.

"Clark, make sure you keep an eye on her," Dr. Roberts ordered.

"I will," Dr. Clark replied.

"Now can we focus on something else?" Dr. Hill said. "I need some of my energy back after such a long day."

Dr. Roberts tapped a few buttons on his phone and then looked up.

The double doors to the lounge swung open, and a young man in a black shirt and black pants with a dark lock of hair over his forehead stepped in, closing the doors behind him. "They're ready whenever you are," he said.

"What about Madam Sherry?" Dr. Roberts asked.

"She's unavailable today," the young man, Alex, replied.

"Tell her to make sure she's here next time."

Alex nodded. "I'll deliver your message," he said.

"Okay, send them in."

Alex turned and threw the double doors open.

Then a large man, whom Alex called Tiny, led the young women in.

orris sat at his desk in his new office and scanned through the information he'd just received. It'd been a long day since receiving the case and digging into it. He'd spent much of the day collecting information, and that had been dreary, mind-numbing work. Morris had been ready to quit for the day.

Then the report had arrived. It had been a pleasant surprise.

Interesting. Who would have imagined this was the identity of the body? This was yet another sign-post that pointed in Zora Smyth's direction. This time, she couldn't deny any knowledge of the victim —it seemed she'd interacted with him long enough that their relationship was common knowledge. It was the kind of circumstantial information he couldn't ignore, even though the history of their altercations wasn't enough evidence on its own to mark her as the killer.

His computer pinged with a new email notification. Morris clicked on the mouse and noticed the email was from the coroner's office.

Just the report he'd been expecting.

He opened the email and scanned its contents. In summary, the cause of the victim's death was heart attack by lethal drug injection, a specific drug only available in the hospital, which meant it was only accessible to medical staff.

Like Zora Smyth.

This was getting better and better. Now all he needed was more definitive evidence, and he could hang the noose around her neck.

"Morris?"

Morris looked up to see Lou, his new partner on the case, poking his head through the door. The skinny young lad he'd known had morphed into a strapping young man with broad shoulders, who'd experienced much on the job and yet kept some of the innocence he'd always had. Working with Lou had been great so far.

"Yes?" Morris said.

"I think you need to hear this."

13

Zora straightened as she finished examining the stoma of the patient lying on the gurney. Angela Davidson, a colorectal cancer survivor who'd had a colostomy a few months ago, had sustained a fall down the stairs this morning and ended up with a sprained ankle. Thankfully, the integrity of the stoma remained intact.

"Let's keep her under observation for as long as orthopedics has her here," Zora told Sally, who'd come down with her from the colorectal unit to the ER. Zora had stopped by to see another ER patient and the nurses had notified her of Angela's case. "Have they seen her?"

Sally shook her head. "Not yet. It seems she arrived right before we saw her."

"Okay, let me know what they decide to do."

"Will do," Sally replied.

Someone swept the curtain aside and entered the cubicle.

Zora turned to see who it was, and her eyes widened. *What is he doing here?*

"Good morning," he said in that accented voice that had stirred something inside her the first time she'd heard it. He made his way toward the other side of the patient.

Then Zora recalled where she was. "What—"

"He's the new trauma attending," Sally whispered from beside her.

Her savior from the airport was a surgeon? Then it registered that he was wearing a medical coat over his green scrubs, the name "Dr. Martin" embroidered over the coat's breast pocket. Who would have thought?

"Good morning," Zora managed to say.

He flashed her a brief smile and then turned to the patient. "How are you doing today, Ms. Davidson?" he said, his attention focused on her.

Zora observed as he chatted with the patient and then examined her. He was gentle yet meticulous. It was also obvious Ms. Davidson had fallen under his spell.

Just like Zora had, it seemed. She should have been on her way out, but she couldn't move.

"He's cute," Sally said quietly from beside her.

That seemed to break the spell, and Zora finally concentrated enough to finish updating her patient notes on her tablet. Once she was done, she stepped out of the cubicle. She had a little time to grab some lunch before a teaching round with first-year and second-year general surgical residents.

"Zora, honey, I've been looking all over for you," a familiar voice drawled.

She turned to see Brian Atkinson, her work BFF, coming to a halt beside her.

"You'll be dead meat if Christina hears you call me 'honey' one more time," Zora said with a smile.

Brian waved her concern away. "I'm sure she's heard me call you that a million times, even before we started dating. You're my first love, you know."

Zora shook her head. "You're crazy. So why the frantic search for *moi*?"

"You didn't answer your phone."

Zora pulled out her phone from her medical coat pocket and checked the screen. There were fourteen missed calls. "What's going on?"

That was when she noticed the nurses giving her furtive glances and whispering to each other.

"Come on." Brian grabbed her arm and led her to an empty cubicle. Then he drew the curtain across it to shut them in and turned to her. "Have you heard?"

"Heard what?"

"Herbert is dead."

The nightmare she'd had flashed before her, and Zora remembered.

It had been Herbert.

The enemy she'd fought, the one she'd recognized. It had been him, and now he was dead.

Nausea rose within her, and she gagged.

"Zora, are you okay?" Brian asked.

Her chest grew tight, and Zora struggled to breathe. "I need fresh air," she said as she swept the curtain aside and hurried out of the cubicle…

… only to see a familiar figure heading in her direction, with someone she didn't know at his side.

Zora's eyes widened. *Detective Morris?* His was the last face she'd expected to see. Wasn't he supposed to be in New Jersey? So what was he doing here? Well, it wasn't her business, since anyone had a right to come to the ER.

Zora waited for him to pass, but he halted in front of her.

"I was told you'd be here," he said.

Her eyes narrowed, her nausea forgotten. He was looking for her? Why?

By now, the hallway had quieted, and all eyes had turned in their direction.

"Zora Smyth?" Detective Morris said with a noticeable gleam in his eyes, which warned her something bad was about to happen. Zora had disliked his arrogant attitude many years ago and could tell her feelings toward him hadn't changed.

She took a deep breath to steel herself. "Yes?" she said, matching his gaze.

"I'm sure you remember me, Detective Morris, from the Lexinbridge Police Department. This is my partner, Detective Gardner. I'm afraid you have to come with us."

This couldn't be happening. "Why?" Zora asked, her pulse already ratcheting up. She forced herself to maintain a blank expression that hid her churning emotions.

He shoved an arrest warrant in her face. "You're under arrest for the murder of Dr. Herbert Johnson," the detective said.

Zora heard the audible gasps from patients and medical staff alike. Hands grabbed her wrists roughly and slapped handcuffs on them.

"Hey!" Brian inched forward, but Zora shook her

head. She couldn't allow him to get arrested for interfering. This was her fight, and she could handle it. He heeded her warning and stepped back.

Morris glared at him for a moment before continuing. "You have the right to remain silent. Anything you say can and will be used against you in a court of law. You have the right to an attorney. If you cannot afford an attorney, one will be provided for you. Let's go."

"I want my lawyer," she said.

Morris said nothing like she'd expected and grabbed her arm. The handcuffs bit into her skin, but Zora ignored the pain.

As he led her away, Zora turned to Brian. *Call Silas,* she mouthed.

Brian nodded his assent and pulled out his phone to make the call.

14

D r. Jason Martin stepped out of Ms. Davidson's cubicle just in time to hear the detectives arresting the doctor. He watched as they led her away.

Dr. Zora Smyth. That was her name. It had surprised him to find out she was a surgeon like him —he hadn't known she was the one when he'd helped her at the airport.

Jason had learned over the years to mind his business. But when he'd seen that thief take off with her wallet, he couldn't help intervening. Jason hadn't known why. He still didn't. The smooth pebble he liked to keep in his pocket had been enough to send the pickpocket buckling to his knees. Thankfully, the thief had had enough sense to leave the wallet behind. Jason had helped, then turned away, never expecting to see her again.

So imagine his shock when he'd sighted her on his first day in the ER. She'd been so engrossed in her work she hadn't noticed him. He'd listened to the gossip from the nurses about how meticulous she was and how much she cared for her patients—something he'd ended up witnessing firsthand over the past few evenings when she'd been on call in the ER.

But Jason had made no move to approach her. In fact, he'd hoped she didn't recognize him.

Jason had moved to Lexinbridge to get away from everything and lead a quiet life—the last thing he needed was anything that would usurp that goal. And what he'd heard so far about Dr. Smyth suggested that would happen if he got entangled with her. It seemed she was a magnet for trouble, and Jason didn't need any of the attention.

He'd heard about the death of Dr. Herbert Johnson. It'd been all the talk during the attendings' meeting this morning, but Jason would have never guessed it had anything to do with Dr. Smyth. She didn't look like she could murder anyone—he had a keen ability to discern folks who were capable of that.

Jason held himself back, though a part of him

urged him to poke around into her issue and find out what the problem was. His philosophy had always been to never poke into anything that didn't concern him, and it had served him well over the years. Besides, he couldn't afford to mess up his entire plan —it could backfire in a way he wasn't expecting.

So Jason forced himself to walk away.

15

Zora stayed silent throughout the ride to the police station, and even when they fingerprinted, photographed, and relieved her of her items. She insisted on her lawyer whenever they questioned her and said nothing else.

By the time Detective Morris led her to a holding cell and shoved her in, Zora guessed it was afternoon.

She stumbled, but remained on her feet as the bars slammed shut behind her. She glared at Morris, but he only ignored her and strode away. Zora had expected them to interrogate her like they had the last time before bringing her here.

Her pulse raced at the sight of the bars in front of her, but Zora willed her heart to slow down. She couldn't afford to panic—she needed all her wits about her to figure out what was going on.

Aside from her, the cell was empty, so Zora moved to the farthest wall and slid down it until she'd drawn her knees up to her chest. The place stank of urine and mold, and Zora fought the urge to gag. But this was precious time to think—only heaven knew what would happen next.

Detective Morris was stubborn, but no fool. The only way he would have arrested her was if he had solid evidence that tied her to Herbert's death. But what could that be? Sure, Herbert had been a thorn in her flesh, but Zora hadn't seen him since she'd heard he'd failed the board exams. Of course, he'd remained at the hospital despite his failure—Herbert was well-connected to the hospital's leadership. But their paths hadn't crossed since then.

So what could have given Morris the audacity to come after her? Why was he so determined to see her go down? Zora could tell his interest in the case was inspired by more than just duty. It was like he had a grudge against her. But why? She'd been surprised to see him in the first place, and she hadn't had any interactions with him since the Formalin Killer case had ended. So why now?

No matter how much she thought about it, Zora

was no closer to finding out what was going on. But she hoped Silas would be here soon—Brian would have contacted him by now. He'd know what to do. So her best plan of action was to do nothing, avoid any kind of trouble, and wait until he arrived.

The bars clanged open, and Zora looked up. A lithe woman with short, spiky hair and a nose ring stepped in. Zora wrinkled her nose when the overwhelming smell of alcohol followed her in. She looked to be in her early twenties and had a baby face that insinuated she couldn't hurt a fly.

But looks could be deceiving, so Zora watched her every move as she wandered over to the other side of the cell and dropped against the wall. The officer who'd brought the woman locked the cell and stepped away and was soon out of view.

Zora lowered her eyes but stayed alert and watched the woman's body in her periphery for any sudden movements. It was better to be safe than sorry.

The next few minutes passed in quiet solitude. The woman had settled on the floor and soon had her eyes closed.

Zora relaxed. It seemed she'd been worried for nothing. She was sure Silas was almost at the station by now.

Then the woman pounced on Zora and bashed her head against the wall.

Zora cried out as she saw stars, and her head felt like it had exploded. Her first instinct was to fight back, but she worried the cops and prosecution wouldn't accept that any punches she threw were in self-defense, given how badly it seemed Morris wanted to take her down. So Zora only lifted her hands to block off the woman's blows and screamed for help at the same time.

But the woman was much stronger than Zora had expected. She rained punches and kicks against Zora's head and body in swift succession, like an experienced boxer taking down an opponent in a knockout round.

At one point, Zora had no choice but to curl into a ball to protect her head and her organs as best as she could. Still, she didn't let up howling as the beatings continued to descend. Even as her body hurt all over.

Yet the punches kept coming.

As if from a distance, she heard the bars clanging open and feet rushing into the cell. At last the blows stopped, and she felt hands pulling the woman off her.

Then Zora passed out.

16

In a mansion nestled in one of the private islands in the Baltic Sea, a nurse, Lila, checked the vitals of the man lying on the bed. They were stable, same as they'd been during the months she'd cared for the man here. Then Lila stretched and massaged the unconscious man's limbs, crooning to him as she turned him to make sure he didn't develop bedsores. He'd become like a friend, one she'd met daily, though she felt certain he wouldn't consider her the same when he woke up. If he woke up.

Through it all, the man didn't stir, and his eyes stayed shut.

She sighed as she tucked a stray strand of her blonde hair behind her ear. Such a handsome young man. What a waste.

Lila had wondered in the beginning what had happened to him, but no one in the villa, not even the bodyguards with big guns who patrolled it, ever said anything—they'd all been paid for their silence. The one gardener who'd broken the rule had disappeared, never to be seen again. Everyone had minded their business since then.

Lila finished attending to him and put away her equipment on a mobile cart that was stashed in a corner of the room when not in use. As she made to roll the cart away to its spot, Lila thought she saw a flicker of one of his fingers.

She froze. Lila watched his hand for several minutes. *Please move*, she prayed. But nothing happened.

She sighed. Maybe it had been a fluke, a figment of her imagination.

Lila turned to leave, and then halted.

There! His fingers had moved again.

This time, Lila waited with her heart in her mouth.

Then it happened again. And again.

Holding back the tears that filled her eyes, Lila reached for the emergency button and pressed it.

17

"What happened?" Captain asked as he glared at Morris. Captain had called him into his office.

Morris forced himself to remain calm—it wouldn't do to agitate Captain further. "I don't understand what you mean, Captain."

Captain rounded his desk and approached him, his nostrils flaring. "You don't understand what I mean? Were you deaf the last time I spoke with you? I asked you to be careful!"

Morris took a step back as he sensed the onset of one of Captain's legendary outbursts. "I was, sir."

Captain pointed a finger at Morris. "Was it careful to arrest her so publicly in front of her colleagues?

And then she almost died in here. In our holding cell, for goodness' sake!"

"I'm sorry, sir."

"Sorry?" Captain got into Morris' face. "Now we have a circus to deal with. Or did you forget about social media? People are saying it's a witch hunt. Morris, are you single-handedly trying to ruin our station's reputation?"

Morris stayed silent. It seemed anything he said would further inflame Captain.

Captain turned back and pounded his hand on the desk. The papers on its surface jumped, and the penholder fell over, spilling its contents all over the desk.

Morris started and took another step backward. It was best not to stay too close when Captain was in one of his moods.

He whirled around to face Morris. "So here's what you're going to do. I know you're pushing for an arraignment tomorrow, but you're going to hold off until Monday and allow the doctors to work on her. To show we care about her health as a citizen."

"Captain!"

Captain's mouth tightened. "Are you disagreeing with me, officer?"

Morris blinked. "No, sir."

Captain paced. "We need to appease the public and show some good faith. Monday is just a few days away. A delay of a few days in the arraignment won't matter if she's guilty. Got it?"

"Yes, sir."

"And stay away from her until then. Don't meet her unless it's absolutely necessary."

Morris's pulse raced. "But Captain, it's my case!"

Captain waved away his concern. "She knows enough not to say anything, anyway. And she has Lawyer Park representing her. Don't give him something he can use to throw out the case."

"Yes, sir."

"Alright, get out of my office." Captain headed back to his swivel chair but then turned and pointed a finger at Morris. "And no more witch hunt."

"Yes, sir."

Captain waved him away, and Morris left the office. His lips tightened as he shut the door behind him.

Because of Zora Smyth, he'd received another dress down. *Well, one more reason to make sure she ends up behind bars where she belongs.*

Morris would obey Captain—he was his superior

after all. But that didn't mean he wouldn't put in the work to find enough rope to hang that blasted doctor.

He couldn't wait for that day to come.

Morris was a man of justice, and Zora Smyth deserved to rot in jail.

18

Zora opened her eyes to see she was lying on a bed in a white-walled room with large windows. She squinted as the recessed light hit her eyes and then opened them wide again as her eyes adjusted.

Where was she?

She tried to turn her neck and gasped at the pain that shot through her body. Every part of her hurt, even bones and muscles she'd never noticed before.

"Thank goodness you're awake," she heard her mom say as her face came into view.

"Where am I?" Zora croaked out. The last she remembered was being attacked in the holding cell.

"In the hospital. Do you remember your name?"

Zora tried to arch her eyebrow but failed. "Mom,

are you trying to be funny?" It was becoming easier to speak, even though it felt like she had cotton balls in her mouth.

Her mom chuckled. "I had to ask." She smoothed Zora's brow. "I was worried. You've been out for a whole day."

Which meant today was Thursday. "How bad is it?" Zora asked as she tried to sit up. But the effort was too much, and she collapsed back on the bed. She wriggled her hands next and sighed in relief. Thank goodness those were fine. Zora didn't know what she would have done if the assailant had damaged her hands and she couldn't operate anymore.

"The doctors say you have a concussion," her mom replied. "Miraculously, there were no broken bones or organ damage, but you have massive bruises all over. And a cut at the back of your scalp that needed a few stitches."

Zora touched her bandaged head. It ached, even though she was sure they'd put her on some painkillers.

"What about the cops?" she asked.

"We're still dealing with the case, but we've got the judge to approve your stay in the hospital for a few days, and it'll take until Monday before you're arraigned. We hope to use the extra days in our favor to find evidence that would help get the case tossed out on that day. In the meantime, the cops are guarding your door, and they've limited your visits to only your doctors and lawyers."

"Do we know what evidence they had for the arrest?"

Her mom shook her head. "They're keeping it close to their chest. But Silas is on it. You know how he is, especially now that he's pissed about what happened to you. He's ready to take that Detective Morris down."

Silas had been Zora's lawyer when she'd first encountered Detective Morris many years ago, and Zora was grateful for him. She, Silas, and Marcus had worked hard to bring the truth to light. Silas had never tried to take Zora's father's place since he started dating her mom, but Zora accepted him in her life for the quasi-father he was. He'd always been there for her whenever she needed him. She pitied the cops who would cross his path.

Her mom adjusted the sheet around Zora. "In good news, we pulled some strings and got Brian assigned as your doctor. He'll be able to carry any messages for you as needed. Also, AJ heard about the arrest and has asked to be included on your legal team."

Zora had met AJ, a lawyer who specialized in wrongful death suits, on her last case when a patient's family had accused her of medical negligence and the subsequent death of the patient. AJ had worked with her to expose the conspiracy behind the case. They'd become close and had had dinner a few times, but Zora had made it clear she wasn't interested in a relationship, so they'd remained friends. "Is it even his area of specialty?" she asked.

"Don't worry about it. He's still a lawyer, and an outside perspective won't hurt. Besides, he's good at ferreting out hidden truths."

"I guess that means Clive is along for the ride." Clive was AJ's investigator, and a very good one at that. He'd performed miracles in finding a missing person on Zora's last case.

"You got that right."

Clive was very much welcome on the team, especially since the only other investigator Zora trusted, Marcus, was dead. *No, this is not the right time to think about Marcus.* "Alright."

"Perfect. I'll add AJ to the legal team," her mom said.

"What's the hospital saying?"

"About your fellowship?" Zora nodded. "Nothing yet. Even your department has given you medical leave instead of making a fuss about your arrest. I guess they're being careful after the hell we raised the last time they withdrew your employment."

That was good to hear. Zora needed to finish her fellowship, no matter what. "What about the woman?"

"The one that assaulted you?"

"Yes."

"They've remanded her into custody for attempted murder. She's staying tight-lipped and has refused to disclose who hired her, but she's insisting she was drunk. Fortunately, Silas and I arrived at the station right as they were hauling her off you, so he got his hands on a copy of the CCTV after a few choice words with the captain. The video was helpful in convincing the judge to let you stay in the hospital."

The corners of Zora's lips lifted. "More like Silas threatened him."

Her mom chuckled. "I never said that."

Zora leaned back into her pillow. Though she wasn't free yet, she was grateful to be in the hospital instead of staying behind bars. She never wanted to go back there. Zora let out a sigh. "We need to solve this case within these three days. I can't go back in there, Mom."

Her mom gave her a determined look. "I'm going to make sure you don't."

And Zora believed it. The mom she knew would do everything in her power to save her. Zora also needed to get cracking on the case, but she was bone-tired and was already feeling drowsy. She yawned.

Her mom brushed her hair away from her face. "You can sleep, dear. I'll be right here."

Zora's eyes closed as her mom continued to stroke her hair. But right before she drifted off to sleep, she heard her mom murmur, "Don't worry, darling. We'll find the real killer, no matter what it takes or how deep they've hidden themselves. But once this case is over, I'm going to sue the police department so hard they'd never think of coming after you again."

19

C lark flinched at the sound of the glass hitting the wall and shattering into a million pieces. He'd called for a meeting this evening as soon as he'd heard the news.

"Why didn't we know he was dead?" Dr. Roberts roared, his face as hard as granite as he scanned the room. The others stared at each other accusingly.

Clark was squirming on the inside, but kept his face stoic. It had shocked him to hear Herbert was dead and murdered at that. "He was supposed to be on vacation in Aruba. Who would have thought—"

"He was right here in town and deader than dead?"

The sound of Roberts' voice grated on Clark's

nerves, but he said nothing. It was all their fault, Roberts included, that they hadn't kept an eye on Herbert. So why was Roberts taking it out on the rest of them?

Lewis twirled his pen. "What if one of us killed him?"

Clark gave him a sharp look. "What do you mean?"

Hill scoffed. "Why would we want him dead when he was making good money for us?"

Allen just stared down at the tablet in his hands. Clark wasn't even sure if his mind was in the room.

"Stop!" Roberts bellowed. "This is not the time for this." He ran a hand through his dark wavy hair that the ladies seemed to love so much. "We need to make sure there is no evidence linking him back to us."

Allen looked up then. "I doubt that'll happen. He was only an errand boy."

Lewis nodded in agreement. "True. He wasn't really one of us. Any information he had would be useless."

Clark agreed with that. The system they'd set up made sure of it.

"So speaking of errand boys, isn't it time we recruited new members?" Hill asked.

Roberts nodded. "I think we should prepare a list," he said. "Even if we delay their recruitment."

"I doubt that's a good idea. I think we need to lie low, given Herbert's death," Lewis said. "We can't afford to have cops sniffing around our business."

"It doesn't matter if we delay or not," Allen said. "We've kept the cops and politicians in our pocket for a time like this."

"What if we continue business as usual, stick to our regular meetings only, and work through who we need to recruit?" Roberts said.

Everyone except Lewis agreed. But his response didn't matter—they'd always gone by the majority rule.

"So that's settled," Roberts said. "Anything else we need to talk about?" No one responded. "Good. What we need now is some relaxation. To get rid of the tension." He pulled out his phone and tapped a few buttons.

The double doors opened, and Alex stepped in. "They're ready for you," he said in a deferential tone and handed a card to Roberts.

Roberts nodded, and Alex led the girls in. The bodyguard with massive limbs who'd come with the girls the last time stayed by the door.

From the corner of his eye, Clark watched as

Roberts slipped out of the room, which meant his preferred girl, Madam Sherry, was around. Sometimes Clark wondered why Dr. Roberts had never allowed the rest of the members to meet her. Maybe he was just being territorial.

But soon Clark's thoughts returned to the present, lost in the ministrations he was receiving from the girl in front of him.

———

Dr. Roberts stood by the floor-to-ceiling windows in a room in the mansion and blew out another ring of smoke from his cigar as he stared out at the dark red hues of the sky. He watched as the setting sun got swallowed into the horizon. Roberts had always liked this view, which was why he brought her here each time. And it was close to his office.

A pair of soft arms encircled him from behind, and Roberts leaned back even as he felt himself stirring to life again. He loved how her innocent angelic face hid the devil she was in the sheets.

From the first time he'd seen her, he'd known she was perfect for him. She'd come with other girls, yet she hadn't behaved like them, as if daring him to take her on. And he'd accepted the challenge.

It had been a wild ride since then, and Roberts had wanted her for himself. When he'd found out he had to share, he'd been less than thrilled.

Roberts was a powerful man, one used to getting whatever he wanted. So today's news hadn't been that unpleasant.

Yet he had to ask. Roberts needed to know she belonged to him completely. He could wait a little more before taking a second spin.

"You've heard Herbert is dead, right?" he asked.

He felt her nod. "Hmmm."

"I hope there are no traces of our association that might link him back to us."

Her arms gave him a squeeze. "Of course not."

"Do you miss him?"

He felt her withdraw a bit, as if insulted. "He was just a client."

His mind appeased, Roberts stood by the windows for a while longer as he appreciated the beauty of the sky. Darkness would soon come like a dark blanket to cover and submerge it. But that was when the stars shone the most—even ones like him.

He took one last drag on the cigar, blew out another ring of smoke, and then turned and dragged Madam Sherry back into bed. The evening was still young, and he wasn't done.

But best of all, Herbert would no longer stand in his way.

———

The surgeon drove into his garage and waited as its door rolled down and closed behind him, plunging the space into darkness. Then he turned off the ignition.

He stepped out of his car, slammed the door shut, and leaned against it as he waited.

She was already here—he could feel her presence and hear her faint breaths.

He'd missed her.

The girls at the club had been good, but they were not her. No one was.

It had surprised him at first when she'd sought his attention. The surgeon wasn't one to open up easily, yet she'd persisted and gotten under his skin. Now he couldn't get rid of her, even if he tried.

And he wanted her.

The surgeon waited, saying nothing. It was up to her to make the first move.

Soon, he felt her arms slip around him from behind. Her rose scent washed over him, and he inhaled deeply. Then he turned and wrapped her in his arms. "I've missed you," he said.

"I've missed you too," she breathed.

That was the other thing he liked about her—she was all soft and feminine in every way.

"How are you feeling?" he asked.

"I don't want to talk about it. I had to see you, but I can't stay. It's too dangerous."

He pulled her closer to him and nuzzled her neck. She let out a sigh. "When can I see you again?" he asked.

She straightened and stared into his face. He could make out her green, almond-shaped eyes. "A week after the funeral."

He didn't like that. "That's a long time."

She lifted her hand to cup the side of his face. "It's for the best," she said. "Don't worry, we'll be together soon."

He had no choice but to accept her words. "Promise?"

"I promise." Then she leaned forward and kissed him. And just when he needed more, she stepped back.

Then he didn't feel her arms again, and the surgeon knew she was gone.

20

Zora had been lying on her side, staring at the darkening sky outside the window, when the door to the hospital room opened. Her eyes darted in its direction, only to see AJ step into the room, holding a slim briefcase by his side.

The stylish lawyer hurried to her, pulled a visitor's chair close, dropped his briefcase at its feet, and sat down. "Hey, how are you holding up?" he said softly.

Zora forced herself to sit up and gave him a small smile. Her body still ached, and she felt a little dizzy, but the nap she'd taken had helped. "I'm alive," she said.

"Thank God for that. Clive sends his regards."

"How's he doing?"

"Antsy to get to work on your case."

Zora chuckled. That was just like Clive. "Thank you." She was glad he was on the case.

His warm eyes held hers. "You're welcome. So how can we help?"

Zora slipped her hand under her pillow and pulled out a small sheet of paper. She'd worked on it after she'd woken up. "This is a list of people I remember were close to Herbert. It might be a good starting point to figure out what happened to him."

AJ accepted the list and scanned it. "Okay, I'll get on it." He folded the paper and tucked it into his suit jacket, then took one of her hands in his. "I know it's difficult in this case, but you have to stay strong, okay?"

She nodded. "I'm fine." Zora was up to the challenge. Then her face turned serious. "But *you* have to be careful. We don't know who we're dealing with, and I wouldn't want anything to happen to either you or Clive."

AJ gave her hand a reassuring squeeze before letting go. "We'll be fine too. I'll let you know once we have something." Then he rose to his feet, leaned forward, and brushed a strand of her hair away from her face. "I have to get cracking on the list. Take care of yourself, okay?"

She nodded. "I will."

AJ gave her a pleasant smile, one that warmed her soul. He was a good friend.

Then he grabbed his briefcase and left the room.

Zora watched as the door shut behind him, then she leaned back and sighed. The short visit had already exhausted her. Zora would need a few days to recover her strength, but time was not on her side.

She lay back down and faced the window again. The darkness in the sky had now swallowed any light that had remained.

But Zora would never give up.

She would bring the truth of Herbert's death to light and save herself, her family, and friends from this nightmare.

21

Christina closed the file she'd been working on and let out a sigh. She should have been off work by now. Christina had one more thing on her list to take care of before she could leave, but she'd found it hard to concentrate since she'd heard the news.

A woman had attacked Zora, and she'd ended up in the hospital.

Christina couldn't believe they'd arrested Zora again. She'd wanted to take emergency leave from work as soon as Brian had called to let her know, but her next patient was a frail old lady who'd taken to Christina when she'd come in for a procedure earlier in the week, and she'd asked for Christina's support during her upcoming appointment. Christina had given her word that she'd be there, and she couldn't go back on it. So she'd stayed the rest of the day and kept a smile on her face.

The other nurses had distanced themselves from Christina like she had fleas as soon as the gossip mill brought news of Zora's arrest. They all knew Zora was her friend. But Christina hadn't cared—Zora was all that mattered to her. Anyone who judged Zora and didn't even doubt for a second that she was the murderer had no place in Christina's life.

"How are you holding up?" a gentle voice said.

Christina looked up to see Dr. Gates standing by her workstation. She hadn't even noticed when he'd arrived in the waiting room. "I'm okay. Staying busy," she said.

"If Dr. Smyth is anything like you, I'm sure she's done nothing wrong," he said.

She gave him a grateful smile. "She's innocent."

"I believe you." A look in his eyes showed he was serious.

"Thank you."

Dr. Gates patted her shoulder. "Hang in there, okay?"

She nodded and flashed him a smile.

Dr. Gates returned her smile and then left the room.

Christina leaned back. She'd never thought that Dr. Gates would be the one to believe her out of all her colleagues—the other doctors pretended like nothing had happened, which hurt even worse than acknowledging the issue.

Her heart felt lighter, and Christina could now focus better. Soon she was done with her last task. Then she packed up her things, said farewell to the nurse on call for the night, left the radiology unit, and headed to the parking lot. Instead of going home, Christina planned to head over to Zora's mom's house and see how she could help. She would spend the night if necessary and head to work from there tomorrow.

Christina reached the garage and took the elevator to the second floor. She'd parked her Mini Cooper at the leftmost corner of the lot—Christina liked the spot since it was far from the elevators and reaching it gave her a chance to stretch and exercise her legs. Soon she arrived at the spot where she'd left her car.

And gasped.

22

Christina watched in muted horror as the cops took photos of her car. The Mini Cooper now looked dilapidated, with dent marks all over it, like the vandal had worked all over it in fury with a hammer, and not like a car she'd only purchased a month ago. The windshield and the rear window lay shattered in pieces, with her tires slashed as well. Whoever had done it had been thorough.

She forced back the tears that filled her eyes. Who would have vandalized her car? Christina couldn't recall offending anyone and knew no one who had a grudge against her. This was one situation she couldn't make heads or tails of.

A hand touched her shoulder, and Christina turned to see Brian, her fiancé, standing behind her.

She let out a sigh of relief as his warm arms enveloped her. "Are you okay?" he asked. He'd been in surgery when she'd called and left a message for him. "I'm sorry about the car," he said as he held her tighter.

"I'll be fine," she said, letting her head fall back against his chest. "Just maybe not now."

"You can cry, you know," he said. Brian pressed a kiss to the top of her head. "I'll make sure no one sees."

Christina let out a shuddering breath. It almost tempted her to take him up on his offer.

"Miss Christina Locke?"

Christina lifted her head to see the detective who'd been called to the case sauntering toward her. Here was a reason she couldn't cry yet. "Yes?"

"Do you have a minute?"

"Of course." She stepped out of Brian's arms but kept hold of his hand. "You can speak freely in front of my fiancé."

"I'm Dr. Brian Atkinson," Brian said to the detective, who nodded his acknowledgment. "Do you know who might have done this?" he asked.

"Unfortunately, there's no way to identify the assailant right now," the detective said to them. "The security camera that covered this section of the parking lot is broken, and none of the other cameras caught anything. Whoever did this knew what they were doing." He flipped the small notebook he'd been holding closed. "We've taken all the photos we need and will file the police report about the vandalism. You can come down to the station for a copy of the report or use this ID number," he handed Christina a small piece of paper, "to request a copy of the report from our website. But please give us twenty-four hours before you do so."

Christina accepted the paper. "Thank you, Detective."

"Do you have any more questions for me?"

"Will you be keeping the case open?"

"Not at this time. But we can certainly reopen it if we find any additional evidence that helps the case."

"Okay, thanks."

"Have a good evening, ma'am." Then the detective turned and left with his team.

Christina ran a hand over her ponytail. She was exhausted—seeing the damaged car had wrung out every bit of her last strength. "I still need to file an insurance claim."

Brian pulled her into his arms. "Okay. We'll take care of it together. Why don't you grab whatever you need from your car? I'll call my body shop guy, and he can come and pick it up. He's reputable and can give you a good estimate on how much the repairs will cost. He can also handle whatever you need to get it up and running. Was there anything missing from your car?"

"No. That's what's so surprising about it, and that's why the cops think it might have been someone with a grudge against me." She nestled further into his arms. "I'm just glad I have comprehensive coverage on my auto insurance policy, otherwise I wouldn't have been able to afford the repairs. It's just upsetting that my insurance rates are going to go up through no fault of mine."

"I can have my guy give you a good quote that's affordable and won't break the bank, if you prefer to cover the costs yourself."

"Really? That might work. Thanks."

Brian gave her another kiss on the head. "You're welcome. Okay, let's grab your things from the car."

Unfortunately, it now meant Christina had to deal with this car business instead of going to Aunt Adrianna's house like she'd planned.

And at the back of her mind, she wondered if this incident had anything to do with Zora's case.

23

"So what do we have?" Adrianna Smyth asked AJ and Silas who sat with her around her dining table. They'd agreed to meet at seven a.m. the next morning at her house. Adrianna had prepared a light breakfast, and now the team had steaming mugs of coffee in front of them.

Adrianna and Silas had cleared their work schedules for the next few days, except for emergencies., and Zora's mom had tasked Alisa with overseeing the office on her behalf. Alisa had protested, since she'd also wanted to help with the case, but her mom had refused to budge on her decision.

"Why don't we start with the upcoming arraignment so we can get that out of the way?" Silas said.

"Okay, I'll go first," Adrianna said. "We've got

Judge Mary Vernon, the same one we had for Zora's arraignment in the past. Hopefully, she'll remain as fair as ever. We have a motion to toss out the case all ready, and one for bail in case we need it. However, we need to know what the DA's office will bring to the table."

"That's what I'm working on," Silas said. "My contact at the police station got a copy of the victim's autopsy report. The cause of death was a heart attack by drug injection, and there was nothing in the report related to Zora, since any number of doctors could have gotten their hands on the drug. But my contact found out something else: they have a witness."

AJ looked up from fiddling with the handle of his coffee mug. "A witness?"

"Yes. The man claimed he saw Zora transfer fifty thousand dollars to her accomplice to kill Herbert."

"That's just ridiculous!" Zora's mom said.

"Is that a joke?" AJ said. "Zora would never do something like that."

"I couldn't believe it myself when I heard it," Silas said.

Adrianna ran a hand through her hair. "And who is this supposed accomplice?"

"My contact couldn't find out who it was," Silas said. "But he's going to keep at it until he does."

"Unbelievable." Then Adrianna's eyes narrowed. "And how did this so-called witness know it was fifty thousand dollars?"

"My contact said the witness claimed he overheard them say the amount," Silas said. "He also stated Zora planned it with her accomplice in such a way that she'd still have a solid alibi in case everything went south."

"And he just decided to be a good Samaritan and showed up," AJ said cynically. "Why now? Why not when he'd overheard someone planning a murder?"

"Witness claimed he was scared Zora's accomplice might kill him," Silas said.

Adrianna raised an eyebrow. "And he won't kill him now?"

"He claimed the accomplice has disappeared. And after he saw the news, he gained the courage to do the right thing," Silas replied.

"Yeah, right." AJ said. He shook his head. "This is absurd."

"I'm surprised the cops believed him," Adrianna said.

"I was as well until I remembered Detective Morris was in charge of the case," Silas replied.

AJ looked from Zora's mom to Silas. "Who is he?"

"A bastard that is still pissed Zora broke his case many years ago," Adrianna said. "He was all set to hang Zora on a serial murder case, only for Zora to turn it around and prove the witness he'd trusted, Alfred Pickles, was in fact the murderer. I guess he never got over the humiliation."

"Ah. One of those," AJ said.

"But it still makes no sense," Adrianna said. "Why would Zora kill Herbert, dump his body in her own car, and then drive around with it in her trunk? That would be stupid."

Silas leaned forward. "That's what I thought, too, but it only gets worse. They found a transfer of fifty-thousand US dollars from Zora's account to an unknown account on the day the witness claimed the deal went down. So even though the scenario looks unbelievable, the judge who signed the arrest warrant couldn't disregard that piece of information."

Zora's mom shook her head. "I don't believe it. You know Zora is as frugal as they come and has never even touched her own trust fund, which means she's been relying on her doctor's salary to get by. Last time I checked, they don't pay residents much, and fellows only fare a little better. I doubt she had up to fifty thousand dollars in her account. Did the so-called transfer come from her trust fund account?"

Silas shook his head. "I called Zora, and she confirmed there was no change to her trust fund. But she got a copy of her checking account's financial records. It appears someone paid fifty thousand dollars via ATM into her account and then transferred it. The person who paid it in wore a baseball cap and evaded the cameras, so there was no way to confirm whether it was Zora or someone else. I have one of our investigators looking into any CCTVs in the area that may have captured the bastard's face."

Adrianna dropped her pen on the table. "Crap." This wasn't looking good for Zora. "Do we know who the witness might be?"

Silas leaned back. "Morris and his partner are keeping that information close to their chests, but my contact is doing all he can to get it."

"Have our investigators found anything at the airport parking?" Adrianna asked.

"Not yet," Silas said. "The CCTV conveniently had a glitch on that day."

"Unbelievable," Adrianna said.

Silas laid a hand on her arm. "But don't worry. We're going through each car that was parked there on that day to see if any of them had a camera that might have captured the events of what happened. It'll take a while, since some owners have retrieved their cars, but we'll track them down. We'll find the evidence, I promise."

"Okay." Adrianna had to believe in her team. She turned to AJ. "Tell me you have good news."

AJ sat up. "Clive and I looked into the backgrounds of Herbert and his known associates according to the list Zora gave me. All the doctors appeared clean. But something else caught our attention and raised a red flag."

"What was it?" Silas asked.

"Once a week, Herbert liked to pass through the Lexinbridge Central Station."

"That doesn't sound so unusual," Silas said. "So he took the train into the city. Lots of folks do that."

AJ leaned forward. "Except he only spends about ten minutes each time before getting out. That's not enough time to take the train and return, even if it was just to the next stop. And this only ever happened on Wednesdays. We caught him on CCTV making the trip, and each time he had a backpack over his shoulder."

"That's interesting," Adrianna said. "Either he was meeting someone there, or—"

"He had a locker there," Silas said.

"Exactly!" AJ said.

Zora's mom took a sip of her coffee. It was bitter,

just the way she liked it. "But how do we narrow that down?"

AJ leaned back, a smug smile on his face. "Luckily, there's a homeless guy who claimed a spot near where the lockers are and busks there. With a little donation and a picture of Herbert, he pointed out which locker Herbert frequented. Clive worked his magic—don't ask me how—and he got into the locker."

Adrianna leaned forward. "What did he find?"

"A little treasure chest," AJ said. "Prescription pills, steroids, you name it, and a ledger with payments made and such. We're still going through the records as we speak. But my guess was that Herbert turned the hospital pharmacy into his personal drug-dealing supply. There were no actual names in the ledger, so we still need to figure out who his clients were."

Adrianna had always thought AJ was a go-getter, and he'd proved it yet again. "Great job, AJ."

AJ beamed. "Thank you."

Silas sank back into his chair. "I can't believe this. This from the same guy that gave Zora such a hard time. Bastard."

"Wasn't he best friends with that other doctor?"

Adrianna said. "The one that was involved in the organ trafficking?"

"Yes," Silas replied. "What was his name again? Grant—no, Graham."

"Yes, that's him," Adrianna said. "What a bunch of losers."

"It seems birds of the same feathers stick together," AJ observed.

Adrianna and Silas both nodded in agreement.

"So it's possible his drug dealings may have gotten him killed," Adrianna said.

"Yes, that's what we're thinking," AJ said. "But we'll keep pursuing other theories too."

"Don't forget to look at his family," Silas said. "There might be something there."

"Will do," AJ confirmed. "And we'll keep working on that ledger."

Adrianna took another sip of her coffee. "So what do we do about AJ's treasure trove? We can't just leave the items in the locker."

Silas had a contemplative look on his face. "We need to ensure the detectives find out about it to cast doubt on their theory that Zora is the killer."

"Which should be fine since we've already taken photos of the contents, made copies of the ledger, and returned everything to the locker the way it was," AJ said.

"Smart man," Adrianna said appreciatively.

AJ blushed. "Thank you," he said.

"I have an idea that might work," Silas said. He leaned forward and explained what he had in mind.

"Hmmm, that should work," Zora's mom said. "It would also make sure an additional pair of eyes beyond the detectives on the case sees those items, so this discovery doesn't get swept under the carpet in case the detectives insist on making Zora the fall guy for the murder."

"I think it's a great idea," AJ concurred.

"So that means we're agreed?" Silas said. Adrianna and AJ echoed their assents.

Adrianna's shoulders relaxed as she considered the idea. "This is going to put pressure on whoever is behind all this, and maybe they'll make a big mistake."

24

Dr. Jason Martin stretched his neck from side to side as he opened his locker in the attendings' on-call room. Last night at the ER had been busy, and he'd been in one emergency surgery after the other. He'd only just finished his last operation, though his night call had ended an hour ago.

Jason had freshened up, and now all he had left to do at the hospital this morning was see his patients in the Trauma unit before he called it a day for a few hours. Then he was supposed to be back at the ER for the cycle to start all over again. His schedule was hectic, but it kept him busy and didn't give him time to think about other matters.

Like Dr. Smyth's arrest.

"Just the man I was looking for," a masculine voice said.

Jason looked up from the scrubs shirt he'd been picking up from his locker to see Dr. Valentine, a fellow trauma attending of his, standing by the doorway that led from the attendings' lounge into the locker area.

"Oh, nice," Valentine said as he stared at Jason. "I wish I had a chest like yours. All the ladies would be all over me for a chance to touch that." Valentine was stout with a soft belly.

If only he knew at what cost, Jason thought. "What's up?" he asked instead.

Valentine moved further into the room until he was leaning against the lockers. "Listen, I need a favor. My wife has her ObGyn appointment this morning, and she's vowed to divorce me if I don't show up. Could you help me check up on Dr. Smyth? You know, the arrested doctor? My fellow, Dr. Atkinson, has been taking care of her, but I haven't seen her as the attending since they transferred her to the VIP floor. I need to leave now before my wife raises hell. Can you help?"

Dr. Smyth? He'd been wanting to know how she was doing, even though he'd done his best to put her out of his mind. Not that he'd been successful so far

—he hadn't forgotten her, not even one bit. Ever since he'd witnessed her arrest, she jumped into his mind and caught him off guard when he least expected it. "Sure, I can handle that," he said.

Valentine gave Jason a friendly punch on the shoulder. "Thanks, man. I owe you one. I'll see you later."

Jason watched him leave and then turned back to don a fresh scrubs shirt and his medical coat. He retrieved his work tablet from his coat pocket, pulled up Dr. Smyth's hospital records, and studied them. Then he tucked the tablet back into his pocket and left the call room.

He took the elevators to the topmost floor where the VIP unit was. Jason figured he'd see Dr. Smyth first before attending to his other patients. Of course, it had nothing to do with the way his heart leaped at the thought of seeing her. What was wrong with him, anyway? Since Dr. Smyth was a magnet for trouble, Jason had to be a sucker for punishment if he was feeling attracted to her.

Jason soon reached her hospital room and waited for the cops guarding her room to confirm with the nurses that he could go in, given he was a new face. Thankfully, Valentine had added Jason's name into the record before leaving, and the verification went through. Then the cops gave him the go-ahead.

He entered the hospital room and slid the door shut behind him. Then he approached the bed. Dr. Smyth's dark hair, beyond the bandage around her head, was splayed out on the pillow, giving her an ethereal look. She was stunning, and that hadn't diminished even with her injuries. Instead, she seemed at peace, unlike how he'd expected her to feel while awake, considering what was going on. Though no IV line was present, a peripheral venous catheter remained on her arm for administering medications.

Her eyes flipped open, clear as day and piercing his soul like she could see every dark corner and crevice of it.

Jason almost staggered back, but caught himself in time, the minute movement hardly noticeable. But he was sure nothing had escaped her eyes.

Zora struggled to sit up as recognition filled her face.

"You don't have to," he said.

But that didn't stop her, and she soon righted herself, adjusting the pillows behind her back, despite the effort it seemed to cost her. "What are you doing here?" she asked in a suspicious tone.

She had to know he wasn't her enemy. "I'm just checking up on you on behalf of Dr. Valentine, who had to step out for an emergency and should be back later today. You're still his patient."

Her shoulders relaxed at his words. Jason didn't know how to interpret that.

"How are you feeling?" he asked.

"Getting better. But my head still hurts a little." She touched her bandaged head.

"Any nausea, vomiting, stiff neck, or seizures?"

Zora shook her head. "Not at all."

"Mind if I do a quick exam?" he asked.

"Sure, go right ahead," she said.

Jason went into full doctor mode and did a quick exam. Most of her bruises had darkened to shades of blue and purple, but thankfully she had no organ damage or broken ribs, despite the severe beating she'd received. She'd been very lucky. The stitches on her scalp also looked to be healing well, and her vitals seemed fine. Dr. Smyth was on her way to full recovery.

Then he covered her with the hospital sheet and stepped back. "Everything is healing nicely," he said. "We should be able to take off that bandage on your head sometime today, but the stitches will remain for the next ten days. We'll also keep you under observation for a day or two before we discharge you."

"Thank you," she said as she readjusted herself back to a sitting position.

"You're welcome." Jason needed to leave now, but he couldn't get his legs to move. "I liked your notes," he blurted out instead.

A look of confusion crossed her face. "What?"

"The patient in the ER… that fell… Ms. Davidson…" For goodness' sake, why was he rambling like a fool?

A smile played at the corners of her lips for a fleeting moment, then disappeared. Jason wished he could see it again. But he had to go. "Okay, I'll get out of your hair now," he said.

Her lips twitched. "My hair? Have you been hiding in it?"

Jason let out a laugh. "Maybe," he teased back. For some reason, he felt comfortable around her. There was something refreshing about her spirit, and even though she was in a horrible situation now, she seemed to have kept her wits about her. Jason had to admit he was drawn to her.

But he wanted to know if she was really okay. "How are you dealing with all this?" he asked.

Her face shuttered, and Jason realized it'd been a

mistake to ask. She might have thought he was the enemy, and he couldn't blame her for being careful. "Anything else, doc?" she said.

"No." He made to leave and then turned back to her. He felt a compulsion to let her know. "I know you didn't do it," he said. Jason had no concrete evidence of this, but he'd learned to trust his instincts, and so far, they'd never steered him wrong.

He didn't wait for her response and left the room.

25

Zora stared out of the window after Dr. Martin left, though she wasn't looking at anything in particular. Why had she driven him away? Dr. Martin had only ever been nice and polite to her, and there had even been a moment there where she'd felt a connection between them. He was new to the hospital and was maybe just trying to make friends. Besides, he'd seemed to have arrived from a flight the same as she had, so chances were low—though not zero—that he'd been the one to set her up. Yet it wasn't Zora's fault—she had to suspect any new person who appeared in her life, especially under unusual circumstances.

But no matter how uncomfortable she felt about how she'd treated him, Zora hadn't called him back to apologize. She couldn't deal with this right now, considering what she had on her plate.

Her mom had stopped by to update her on the progress they'd made, but not before having one of her investigators do a sweep of the hospital room for bugs. Fortunately, there'd been none. But Zora had understood the need for it—they couldn't be too careful.

It had shocked her to hear about Herbert's stash. Herbert had been careless with patients, and Zora had had little patience for him as a doctor, but that didn't mean she'd wished him dead. Now it seemed he'd gone further into the dark side than she could have imagined. Little wonder he'd ended up dead.

But now her team needed to unravel the case faster than ever, since time was running out before the arraignment, before Zora ended up in a tight noose that had no place being around her neck. It sucked that she couldn't be more hands-on in solving the case, but she was determined to help in any way she could. So Zora spent the next few minutes thinking about how she could do just that.

Her phone vibrated.

Thankfully, she had access to it here. She was sure her phone records were being tracked, but fortunately, they couldn't listen in. The scramblers her mom had installed in the room made sure of that.

Zora pulled her phone from under her pillow and swiped the answer button. "Hey, AJ. What's up?" she said.

"I believe your mom has told you about the ledger we found?"

Zora's mom had indeed done so. "Yes," she replied.

"We found entries in it marked 'GSC' spread out over a couple of months. We can't seem to figure out what it means, and Clive suggested it might be a hospital-related acronym. Do you have any ideas what it might stand for?"

GSC… GSC… Something about the letters tugged at the back of her memory. She'd heard the initials before. But where? *Think, Zora, think.* Not that it was an easy feat, considering how much her head hurt with the effort. But she couldn't give up.

Then it came to her.

She'd heard them at the welcome dinner held as part of the fellowship orientation a month ago. The surgery department had hosted one, and both Zora and Brian had attended. Zora had been standing with other fellows at a corner of the room before the dinner began, and they'd seen Dr. Clark laughing with Dr. Hill, an attending in the plastic surgery unit. Someone behind her had commented that both Dr. Clark and Dr. Hill were members of the GSC. Zora had asked what the acronym meant, and another fellow had confirmed it as "The Gentlemen Surgeons Club," some sort of prestigious old-boys' club. It had seemed the other fellows had wanted in on it.

"The Gentlemen Surgeons Club," Zora said excitedly.

"Gentlemen Surgeons Club? Do you know more about it?" AJ asked.

"No, I don't, but I know someone who might." Brian was a fountain of information of this type and might know. "I'll call you back."

Zora disconnected the line and called Brian. "Hey, bestie," Zora said.

Brian chuckled. "What's up?" Brian had already checked in on her in the early hours of the morning and had told Zora about the vandalism. Zora had spoken with Christina, who'd assured her she was fine.

"Do you know anything about the GSC, the Gentlemen Surgeons Club?"

"Why do you ask?"

"It has something to do with Herbert."

Brian thought for a moment. "It's a club that was

formed by some surgeons in this hospital many years ago. Very exclusive, and you can only join by invitation. I've heard they meet regularly, but I'm not sure where. Does it have anything to do with Herbert's death?"

"I don't know. We're just trying to understand him and following up with any clues, even if it leads nowhere."

"If he's part of the club, I can see why," Brian said. "We both know Herbert was well-connected."

"Well, yeah, but we're not sure if it's even that. It might just be a fluke. Anyway, thanks for the information."

"You're welcome. I'll talk to you later."

"Alright." The line went dead.

Zora then called AJ back and told him what Brian had said. "And I think Dr. Clark and Dr. Hill are members of the club," she finished.

"This is very helpful," AJ said. "Maybe if we follow Dr. Clark and Dr. Hill around, we can find out where the club meets. Clive is very good at getting that kind of information."

"I bet," Zora said. She'd seen firsthand how Clive had tracked down someone who'd set her up on her last case and who'd been determined to stay hidden.

AJ chuckled, and then his voice turned serious. "How are you holding up?" he asked.

Zora stifled a sigh. What was it about this question that everyone loved asking it? Yet this was AJ, and he only meant well. "As well as I can be, given the circumstances."

"We'll make sure this is over soon," AJ promised.

Zora appreciated his support and faith in her. "Thanks for helping. I'm sorry you got caught up in all of this."

"That's what friends are for. It was my choice, remember? You can pay me with a dinner after this is over."

Zora smiled. AJ, always angling for a dinner. "It's a deal."

"Great. Okay, let me get this information over to Clive ASAP."

"Alright. But be careful. We don't know who we're dealing with."

"I will be. And you too, okay?"

"I'll do the same. Bye." Zora ended the call.

She slipped her phone under her pillow and leaned back.

Something told her they were headed in the right direction with the case, though she wasn't sure what they'd find.

But the uncertainty didn't mean she was ready to give up.

Given how much Detective Morris was pushing the case, Zora prayed they'd be able to turn the tide soon before the detective carried out his twisted vengeance.

26

Detective Morris fended off the cameras that were shoved into his face as he flashed his badge and crossed the police cordon that blocked off the locker area at Lexinbridge Central Station. Lou followed closely behind him.

"How did this leak?" he asked through gritted teeth.

"I don't know," Lou replied. "We only just received the information ourselves not too long ago."

Morris strode through the space until he arrived in front of the locker. He glanced around. "Where's the person in charge?"

"I'm here," a small man in an orange and brown uniform replied. He'd been standing a few feet away and now stepped in Morris' direction.

Morris flashed a warrant in his face. "Open it."

The man unclipped a bunch of keys from a hook at the waist of his pants, selected a key, and slid it into the keyhole of a locker in the upper section. Then he opened the locker.

The flashes and clicks from the cameras behind him increased, but Morris ignored them.

Morris saw the locker held an array of pill bottles, drug packets, and ampoules in various transparent freezer bags, all filled to the brim. A closer look revealed most of them were prescription drugs.

He grimaced. What had that dead doctor been up to? This looked like the set-up of a serious drug operation, the last thing he'd expected. Just as he was about to call the police photographer over, he noticed a black notebook at the back of the pile.

Morris donned a set of gloves and picked it up. It looked like a journal, but when he flipped through it, he noted annotations and symbols throughout the book—it had to be a ledger or a black book. Morris couldn't make out what the initialisms meant, but he was certain it related to the drug operation. He replaced the notebook where he'd found it and then called over the photographer, who then set about capturing pictures of the evidence. Once he was done, Morris pulled out an evidence bag, picked up the notebook, and dropped it into it before tucking the bag into his jacket.

He turned to the photographer. "Make sure no one gets their hands on these photos."

The photographer nodded and then stepped away.

"Let's get all these bagged and entered into evidence," Morris told Lou. "And get a copy of the CCTV."

"On it," Lou said and left to do as asked.

Morris took one last look at the locker area and then headed toward the cordon's exit.

As he left the train station's entrance and reached his car in the parking lot, Morris swore under his breath and kicked his tire. The case had just gotten more complicated. If he couldn't prove Zora was part of the drug ring, the defense could cast reasonable doubt on Zora Smyth as the killer, which could enable her to slip the net.

The case had only gotten worse. And now it seemed like what they'd just discovered was only the tip of the iceberg.

27

Roberts looked up from where he sat at his desk in the mansion's library. He'd claimed the space for his own, as all his predecessors had done. "I thought we agreed to only convene at our regular meetings," Roberts growled. "What are you doing here?" He'd come by to get some paperwork for the club done, but that was his usual practice.

Clark wrung his hands. "I think someone was following me."

Roberts rose to his feet and came around the desk. "And you brought them here? Are you insane?"

"I didn't—"

"—think, did you?" Roberts could see the guy was falling apart at the seams.

Clark ran a hand through his hair. "I don't know. I just feel like someone's been watching me."

Roberts reached forward and gripped Clark's arms. "Get a hold of yourself. If you keep fretting like this, you'll draw attention to yourself and then to us."

Clark shook off Roberts' hands and rubbed his arms as he paced. "I heard they found something… documents. What if any of those lead to us? I can't lose everything!"

"They found drugs and only a few receipts. Nothing related to us."

Clark looked at him in disbelief. "Are you sure?"

"Of course I'm sure. Everything is fine."

"Okay." Clark took a deep breath. "Okay, every-thing will be fine." He grinned. "It will be fine." He ran a hand through his hair. "I need a drink." He grabbed a glass from the tray of drinks on the corner of the large desk, poured himself a shot, and downed it.

Roberts patted Clark's shoulder. "Why don't you relax here for now? I'll be right back." Clark nodded and flopped onto the black couch in the space and closed his eyes. Roberts moved further into the library between the floor-to-ceiling bookshelves until he reached the door to the adjoining room and stepped through it.

"I think he's losing it," a voice said. The speaker in question, Alex, was leaning against the wall right past the door. Roberts' and Alex's families had done business in the club for many years and knew each other's secrets. They'd been discussing business before Clark barged in, so Roberts had sent him here. "We can't trust him."

Roberts stayed silent and patted his jacket for his cigar, then remembered he'd left it on his desk in the library when he'd forgotten that cigars and centuries-old books didn't mix. That was the only disadvantage of working in the library.

"I think we should get rid of him before he becomes more trouble than he's worth," Alex insisted. "He seems to have calmed down now, but once he's back out there, nothing is going to stop him from making a mistake. You need to do what's best for the club."

Roberts closed his eyes for a moment. He wasn't a killer, but as the head, he'd known and had been told certain occasions might demand desperate measures. Clark was one of his oldest friends, but Roberts had to think on behalf of everyone and do what was best for the greater good. It was his responsibility to make sure the club remained unharmed.

He straightened and then nodded. Alex would figure out how best to get rid of him.

Then Roberts walked back through the doorway and into the library to chat with his friend for the last time.

28

Patrick Shreeve, also known as Paddy, sat in his car in the dark and waited. He'd gotten a call for help from his old buddy Clive, so here he was.

Clive and Paddy had served in the army together, and though Clive liked to touch base with him now and then, it'd been a few months since Paddy had heard from him.

Paddy had only recently hung up his own private investigator shingle. After his honorable discharge from the army, he'd lent out his investigative skills as a favor to friends, including a former neighbor who'd wanted to find out if her husband of twenty years was cheating on her, and a cousin who'd asked for help to track down his show dog, whom Paddy found out had been stolen by a competitor. Paddy couldn't say he was exceptional at being a PI, but he got by. But since he'd started his business and taken on more jobs, the money had become a nice supplement to his VA benefits.

So the request from Clive had been right up his alley. Tailing Dr. Clark all day had been boring, and it had surprised him when Clark had rolled up to the estate. Paddy was now waiting—parked in an inconspicuous corner—for him to come out of the mansion.

He glanced around his surroundings with its massive houses, perfectly landscaped gardens, and expensive cars. Paddy had never been in this part of town before—the area had always been too rich for his blood. He'd have loved to explore it, but that didn't seem like a good idea. Paddy was already sticking out like a sore thumb with his grey regular SUV—most cars that had driven by cost millions. Besides, who knew what security system these rich folks had in place to track people like him? Clive had asked him to stay out of sight, and that was what he planned to do.

The mansion's massive gates opened, and the red Aston Martin he'd been waiting for slipped out. Paddy trailed him, and like he'd expected at this time of the day, Clark went straight home to the address Clive had given Paddy as his place of residence. The home was yet in another wealthy part of town, though not as ostentatious as the place they'd just left.

The house was dark as Clark drove into the garage. After a few minutes, Paddy saw the light come on through a window on the upper level. He guessed it was Clark's bedroom.

Paddy sat in his car and observed as the shadows of the man moved about for a while. Then the light went out. Paddy assumed Clark must have gone to bed.

By now, it had become very dark, and the street-lights had turned on.

Paddy figured it was time to leave. The last thing he wanted was to draw any attention from the neighbors, which might lead to him having to explain to the cops what a wounded veteran, with a penchant for the pubs on the outskirts of town, was doing in this neighborhood.

Besides, Paddy had a date with Lizzy from the diner he frequented. He'd been on the widow's case for years, and she'd finally agreed to watch a late-night movie with him. He had to leave now if he wanted to make it. Paddy couldn't afford to mess up this one shot.

He pulled out of his spot and into the street. He'd update Clive later tonight once his date with Lizzy was over. Or in the morning if his luck stayed good.

Soon Paddy headed out of the area as fast as he could go without breaking speed limits, barely missing a hit from a van with tinted windows that was headed in the opposite direction.

29

Detective Morris stared down at the naked man lying in the bathtub. One of his slashed wrists hung off the edge, and blood ran down the side of the tub and onto the marble floors. Otherwise, everything else in the space seemed pristine—too clean if he thought about it.

Morris turned away from the scene, left his team, who were taking pictures, and headed to the doorway where he met Lou. They'd only been called to this case when Captain had realized the victim was a surgeon at Lexinbridge Regional. He'd wanted Morris to confirm if the death had connections to the Herbert case.

"Who called it in?" Morris asked.

"His wife," Lou replied. "She found him this

morning after she returned from a trip to visit her mom."

"Where is she?"

"She collapsed, and they took her to the hospital."

"We'll need to speak with her. And we've established she really visited her mother?"

Lou nodded. "Her mom is at a nursing home in Boston, and the CCTV footage they sent us confirmed she was with her. We also found a suicide note on the bed." He showed Morris a letter he'd placed in a transparent evidence bag.

Morris accepted it and read the note. It said something about being depressed and being tired of life. It sounded generic, and not what he'd expect from a doctor of his caliber. And why would the man commit suicide? From his brief look around the house, he gathered things were going well for the doctor.

"Did you find anything else he's written?" Morris asked. Having encountered his share of homicides covered up as suicides, Morris needed to be sure that Dr. Clark had written the note. In a well-forged suicide note, the handwritings may appear the same, but the tone of the note and mannerism of writing would vary. So a handwriting analysis could confirm if the note was fake or real.

"Here." Lou showed him a sheet of handwritten research notes. "I found it in the desk drawer in his study."

Morris compared the sheet to the suicide note. The two seemed similar, yet there was a subtle difference. Dr. Clark was more upbeat even in his research notes, yet the suicide note read flat and stiff. The doubts he had about the suicide grew bigger. "Let's get these to the handwriting experts." He handed both items to his partner.

"On it."

"Also check if there's any relationship between Herbert and this Dr. Clark." He thought for a moment. "And between Zora Smyth and Dr. Clark."

"Will do." Lou left and headed out of the house.

Morris looked back in the bathroom's direction. Another doctor was now dead. It looked like a suicide, but Morris didn't buy it. Even though he still held onto his belief that Zora Smyth had a hand in the death of Dr. Herbert, he couldn't help thinking she couldn't have had anything to do with Dr. Clark's death, though he still planned to check with the cops guarding her hospital room to confirm she'd been there all this time.

Two dead doctors from Lexinbridge Regional. What was going on in that hospital?

30

"Zora, you need to see this." Brian handed his phone to her. He'd stopped by to see her on his morning rounds.

"What is it?" Zora said as she accepted the phone. She was sitting up against the bed's headboard.

"Look."

She scanned the report on the screen. They'd headlined it "Prominent Doctor Commits Suicide." She gasped as she saw the name on it. "Dr. Clark? How?"

Brian sat down on the bed. "I don't know. I saw him a few days ago, and he didn't seem suicidal to me."

Then Zora remembered the conversation she'd had with Clark a few days ago. "Give me one second." She dialed AJ's number. It rang once, and then the line connected.

"Hi, Zora," AJ said.

"Hey. Did you see the news about the doctor who committed suicide? Dr. Clark?"

"I did. Hold on. I'm here with your mom and Silas. Let me put you on speakerphone."

"Hello, dear," her mom said.

"Mom. Hello, Silas," Zora said.

"Hey, Zora," Silas said.

Brian tapped Zora's arm and mouthed that he'd be right back. Then he stepped out of the room.

"Yes, we all saw the news report," AJ said. "Clive had someone tailing him for most of yesterday, and the individual reported Clark had gone to bed for the night before he'd left. There'd been no one else in the house."

"We're finding it hard to believe it was suicide," Silas said. "A man who wants to commit suicide doesn't go to bed first, especially when he's all alone and could have done it at the time if he wanted. My contact at the station says the estimated time of death was somewhere between one a.m. and three a.m."

"But why did you bring him up?" Zora's mom asked.

"That Dr. Clark," Zora began. "I spoke to him a

few days ago. I noticed he'd ordered some extra unnecessary tests for a patient, and when I approached him about it, he almost bit my head off. Now he's dead. Do you think he might have been involved in some sort of hospital fraud and got killed for it? He didn't look depressed to me or like someone contemplating suicide."

"You might be onto something there," AJ said. "Do the initials XY, CN, or MI mean anything to you? Those were the most common annotations in Herbert's journal after GSC."

Zora thought for a moment, and then a light bulb went off in her head. "Could it be XY for Xray, CN for CT Scan, and MI for MRI?"

"Sounds very plausible to me," Silas said.

Zora's mind raced. She could tell this was an important clue that could help them decode what was going on. "So what if there was some sort of ongoing hospital fraud related to these tests?"

"That would make sense," AJ said. "And maybe Herbert was part of it. Maybe the other abbreviations we've found are related to other tests, too. I'll get this information over to Clive ASAP." Zora heard the scraping of a chair against the floor and then fading footsteps.

"Good thinking, Zora," Silas said.

"Thanks," she replied.

"Zora, I have bad news," her mom said.

Zora's heart rate quickened. "What is it?"

"The prosecution requested a change in the judge, and the court granted it. We now have Judge Weston for the arraignment. We filed a motion to get him to recuse himself, since he favors the DA's office, but they denied it."

Zora leaned back. It wasn't the news she'd expected to receive, but it was only a minor setback. It didn't mean they couldn't still get the case tossed out. Even proving a link between Dr. Clark's and Herbert's deaths would cast further doubt on the case and help them. But the body found in her trunk and the money from her bank account were still going to be the hardest evidence to refute. "Okay. Any break-throughs regarding the airport parking lot?"

"Not yet," Silas said. "But we're following up a lead we think might pan out. Hang in there, okay?"

"Will do." Zora heard a phone ring in the background.

"Zora, we have to take another call," her mom said.

"Alright. I'll let you guys go."

"We'll talk later, dear. I love you."

"Love you too, Mom."

The hospital door slid open, and Zora looked in its direction.

Her heart sank.

It was Detective Morris and his sidekick. Zora had known they'd check in, but she'd hoped they wouldn't. Morris' arrival was never good news. A guard said something to Morris, and he turned to answer him.

"Silas, do you think you could get to the hospital?" Zora said in a whisper. "The detectives just walked in."

"I'm on my way," Silas replied. "Don't talk to them until I get there."

"Okay." Zora ended the call. She slipped the phone under the pillow and hoped Morris hadn't seen it. Though she could use it, she didn't see any reason to flaunt it in his face. He might just be vicious enough to revoke the permission.

She watched as they approached her bed.

"Zora Smyth," Morris said.

Zora realized he'd never called her Dr. Smyth. *He must think I'm still the young medical student he'd encountered many years ago. What an idiot.* "Hello, Detective," she said as she maintained a calm affect.

They stopped a few feet from her bed. "We have some questions for you," he said.

"I want my lawyer present," Zora responded.

"It won't take long," Morris said and plowed ahead. "Did you know a Dr. Clark?"

Zora stayed silent. He did not know she was wise to the ways of the police.

"We discovered you argued with Dr. Clark a few nights ago. What was that about?"

Breathe in, breathe out. Keep it steady, Zora thought to herself. It was time to dwell on something else, to resist the temptation to respond. She ran a mental checklist on the next surgery she was supposed to have handled if they hadn't arrested her. *Make an incision, apply retractors…*

"Dr. Smyth, Dr. Smyth. Can you hear me?"

Ah. So he'd now decided to call her that. Did it mean he was having a change of heart about the case?

She opened her eyes to see Morris with a look of annoyance on his face. *Probably not.*

"Dr. Smyth, you'll have to speak with us soon."

"I invoke my right to counsel." There. She'd spoken. Was he satisfied?

A nurse with her blonde hair in a bun wheeled in a mobile cart at that moment.

Thank you, God, Zora thought.

She soon reached Zora's bedside.

"I'm sorry, but could you please wait outside?" the nurse said to the detectives in a polite but firm voice. "I need to attend to my patient."

Zora could tell Morris wasn't happy at the interruption. "We'll be back," he said.

The nurse waited until Morris and his sidekick had left the room and then adjusted Zora's pillows. "Christina saw the detectives entering the elevators and called me to check on you," the nurse said. "Don't worry, we'll not let them harass you on our watch. I'll check your vitals in a bit and then let them know you're asleep and need your rest."

Zora beamed at her. "Thank you." That would keep them away, at least until Silas got here.

The nurse returned her smile. "You're welcome."

Then Zora laid back and closed her eyes. Thank goodness for Christina.

Zora just hoped her current situation wasn't affecting Christina's work.

Christina scanned the notes on the computer screen in front of her. She was on a day call with one of the other nurses, even though it was a Saturday and she hadn't been in the unit that long.

This can't be right, she thought as she stared at the notes. She'd been in the room when Ms. Perry had undergone the interventional radiology therapy for her osteoarthritis. At the start of the procedure, Christina had clarified with Dr. Gates what injections Ms. Perry would receive, and he'd assured her he'd inject only the hyaluronic acid derivatives into her knees. And that was what Christina had witnessed. The patient hadn't received intra-articular corticosteroids. Then why did the notes say she'd received both?

Christina rose from the nursing station where she'd been working and headed over to the medications room. She swiped her ID card on the card reader and entered the space. Christina headed to the secure metal cabinet and punched in the combination code, which the unit updated on a weekly basis. Then she inserted the key and unlocked the cabinet.

She checked the quantity of corticosteroids that were available. It appeared to be short by one unit, though she'd accounted for them all at her last count after the procedure. The records seemed perfect, as it now matched Dr. Gates' notes. Since no other patient had needed the drug since then, where was the missing ampoule?

Christina rubbed her forehead. Could she have been mistaken? *No!* She was sure of what she'd witnessed during Ms. Perry's procedure, which meant Dr. Gates could have made a mistake in his notes. But the only way to be sure was for Christina to confirm it with him.

She relocked the cabinet and left the medication room. Then she strode over to the radiologists' lounge, knocked, and poked her head in. Dr. Gates was the only one in the room and looked up from the journal he'd been reading at the conference table tucked into a corner of the room.

He smiled. "Yes, Nurse Christina?"

"Do you have a minute?" Christina said.

"Sure. Come on in."

Christina entered, leaving the door ajar. Though she was sure she had nothing to fear from Dr. Gates, it was her personal policy to leave doors open during such conversations. She also didn't need any weird rumors of them alone in a closed room floating around the hospital.

"So, how can I help you?" Dr. Gates said pleasantly.

"I have a question," Christina said. "It's about Ms. Perry's procedure."

"Go on. What about it?"

Christina held his gaze. "You noted she received both HA and corticosteroids, but I believe she only received HA. You mentioned during the procedure that she'd get the corticosteroids a few weeks later."

The expression on Dr. Gates' face didn't change. Instead, he leaned back. "Oh. That must have been an oversight. Ms. Perry was considering the corticosteroid injection right before leaving, but then changed her mind. I'm sure it's somewhere in the intervention room. Thanks for bringing it to my attention. I'll take care of it."

Christina's shoulders relaxed. It had only been a mistake. Thank goodness she hadn't made a big deal out of it.

"Anything else?" Dr. Gates asked.

Though he stayed pleasant, Christina felt a chill in the air that hadn't been there before. "That's it," she said. "Thanks. I'll leave you to it."

Christina crossed the room, exited, and closed the door behind her.

———

Dr. Ethan Gates heard another knock right after Christina left, and he glanced in the door's direction as it opened. He tensed as Molly, the janitor, entered, bearing a mop. She closed the door behind her and began to clean the floor of the lounge.

"She almost exposed you," she said, annoyance written all over her face.

It was in moments like this that Ethan hated her. He couldn't recall what he'd seen in her in the beginning, but now he couldn't even cut her off, since she'd burrowed her way deep into his life. If Ethan tried to leave, Molly's brother would kill him.

Ethan had only been a small-time crook, fencing items here and there, until he'd met Molly. Molly had introduced him to the world of prescription fraud. She'd seemed cute, and he'd tolerated her then, which was why he'd gone along with the jobs she'd suggested. That was when Ethan discovered he had a knack for all things medical. He could memorize all the medical terms and their meanings, and he understood the procedures after only watching their videos once. Ethan had been a child of the streets and had only attended school for a short time before dropping out, so he'd never recognized the gift he had.

Molly and her brother had been so excited about the discovery, they'd created a fake persona for Ethan with all the right records and licenses. Suddenly, Ethan had become a radiologist. They'd paid a high price for the persona, too. The brother-sister duo had recognized the big bucks were in diagnostics fraud. Ethan had shadowed a radiologist with a revoked license and who now worked underground. He'd gotten good with the procedures and terms.

He became a genius doctor without a genuine license within a year.

Then they'd started their operation. Ethan appeared at the first hospital, a run-down general hospital, and plied his skills. They'd chosen the hospital since it hadn't yet digitized its medical records-keeping, so it'd been easy to manipulate his records to show he'd worked there for a much longer time than he had. The local authorities shut the hospital down not long after, but by then Ethan had already moved to another hospital with his new work history.

From then on, he spent six months to a year at a time in each hospital before transferring to another. This gave Ethan a plausible work experience without having to stay long enough for them to find out what he'd been up to. Ethan had become adept at including additional procedures and therapies his patients hadn't received in their patients' notes and getting paid for them based on the fee-for-service model that hospitals employed in reimbursing radiologists. With each hospital, he'd set financial targets and left once he'd exceeded those goals.

Ethan hadn't met his target at Lexinbridge Regional yet, and his goals this time around would enable him to take some time off to travel, enjoy his wealth, and cut the umbilical cord that bound him and Molly together. He wasn't greedy enough to think his streak of luck would last forever. Federal jail held no appeal for him.

"It's fine," Ethan said. "We only have a few weeks left here."

Molly straightened, a petulant look on her face. "I think we should leave now. You heard about the doctor that died."

Ethan fought to hide his irritation. Yes, he'd heard about the doctor's death, but it had nothing to do with him. "We have to reach our target. You know that."

"I don't trust her," Molly replied.

Ethan had noticed her jealous attitude whenever Christina was around.

He'd heard someone had vandalized Christina's car and had known Molly was the culprit. Yet he couldn't confront her—she'd only deny it, and calling her on it might have inspired her to do something worse. But Molly didn't know him hanging around Christina was the only thing that made him not snap at her. That was how much he'd tired of her.

Ethan had never thought he'd fall for the redhead, yet he had. She was funny, genuine, and even with the news about her friend, she'd held her head high. But letting Molly see his feelings would only mean bad news for Christina. Molly's jealousy had no limit. That was why he'd tried to stay far away from Christina. Yet sometimes he couldn't resist. Still, staying at Lexinbridge Regional until he met his goals would give him more opportunities to see her before he had to leave for good. He couldn't let Molly take that away from him.

Of course, he'd been able to succeed faster at Lexinbridge Regional because of that club. Ethan had uncovered their activities as he'd laid down his own, but instead of reporting them, he'd offered to partner with them and show them how to better hide their work. They'd agreed, and the partnership had worked well so far. Now Ethan got his pre-approvals faster and his payments processed quicker because of the club's connections at the insurance companies. In exchange, he gave up a percentage of the proceeds.

Molly's brother had pushed for the group to accept Ethan as a member. He thought it'd give them some respectability, but Ethan knew that would never happen. The group considered themselves high above his station and viewed him as a parasite they'd get rid of when they no longer needed him. But they were all thieves, just like him. He had his own plans for the future, and they didn't include the club or anyone else.

"We'll leave as planned," he said. "There's no sense in changing tracks now."

Molly glared at him for a moment, then picked up the mop and left.

Ethan's shoulders relaxed. He'd won the battle and dodged the bullet.

Now all he had to do was be more careful, and he'd taste his freedom soon.

Christina stifled a yawn as she exited the elevators on the parking level. The hot sun had cooled off somewhat, for which she was glad.

She'd been lucky that the nurse on the next shift had arrived early. With a speedy handover and no patients waiting in the wings, the nurse had encouraged Christina to leave early and enjoy her weekend. Now Christina could go shopping for some much-needed groceries—she hadn't had time to do so since they'd vandalized her car.

Brian's body shop guy had offered her a hard-to-beat deal that Christina couldn't turn down. She even suspected Brian had paid him the difference behind her back to make the offer palatable to her. Since he'd only meant well, Christina had feigned ignorance and taken the deal.

Now she approached the rental Lexus hybrid the mechanic had given her to use in the meantime. Christina had changed her parking spot after the incident and moved closer to the stairwell exit, so it only took a few steps from the elevators before she reached her car.

As she unlocked the door, she spied a sheet of paper sticking out from under her windshield wiper.

Christina leaned forward, pulled it out, and opened it.

The words, "Leave Dr. Gates alone. He's mine. Or else…," handwritten in a bright red marker, leaped out at her from the sheet.

She stared at the paper for a moment. Only one person came to mind as she wondered who might have written the note.

The janitor whose name she'd found out was Molly.

Christina had felt Molly's eyes on her whenever she came to clean the waiting room, and she hadn't liked the lady any better than the first day she'd met her. But Molly had done nothing else since then.

Until now.

Christina had seen her lurking outside Dr. Gates' office as she'd left, though Molly had tried her best to stay hidden. Her displeasure at Christina had been clearly written all over her face.

However, Christina had had enough. She wasn't scared of Molly, but the stress wasn't worth her time.

It seemed being friends with Dr. Gates—even if it was only within the confines of the work environment—was more trouble than it was worth. It was best to avoid them both. Thankfully, Christina had no more scheduled procedures with Dr. Gates for the rest of the month. She'd do her best to make sure she wasn't scheduled with him for the next month, either.

Christina needed no extra drama in her life.

Zora's troubles were already more than enough for both of them.

Zora sat up when Silas arrived, dressed impeccably as usual and holding his lawyer briefcase. The detectives followed him in— they must have been waiting outside. Zora had called Silas after the detectives had left the first time and updated him on what had happened.

Silas grabbed one of the visitor's chairs, sat down, and motioned to the detectives to take the remaining seats. Morris and his sidekick remained standing.

He crossed his long legs. "What would you like to know?" he said.

"Dr. Smyth, what was your relationship with Dr. Clark?" Morris asked.

"What is this about?" Silas said. "Is my client being charged with another crime?"

"We just want to understand Dr. Smyth's relationship with Dr. Clark," the detective replied.

Silas flicked off an imaginary lint from his suit. "My client is not obliged to answer any questions and has made it clear she will not do so." Silas sighed. "Detective Morris, you know better than to harass my client after she's invoked her right to counsel," Silas said with a hint of rebuke.

Morris' jaw clenched so hard Zora worried his teeth might crack. "We'll be back, Dr. Smyth," he said. Then he left with his sidekick behind him.

"That was quick," Silas said. "I thought he'd push some more."

Zora nudged his shoulder. "You love it, don't you? This whole back-and-forth with the cops."

"I can't say that I don't. There has to be a silver lining somewhere in this whole situation. But you can be rest assured he won't be back anytime soon."

"So how's Mom doing?"

"You know how she is. She'll never give up where one of her cubs is concerned. We wouldn't want her to."

"I know. Thanks for being there for her."

Silas gave her a warm smile. "There's no other place I'd rather be."

"So when are you two tying the knot?" she asked.

Zora thought she'd never see the day when Silas blushed, but here he was, his ears turning all red.

"Whenever she's ready," he said. "Does this mean I have your approval?"

Zora flashed him a smile. "You're good for her, and that's all that matters."

He took her hand in his. "Thanks so much, Zora. This means a lot." He released her hand. "But first we need to get you out."

"How's that going? You can tell me the truth. You know I can handle it."

Silas looked her in the eye. "Zora, we're going to make sure you're released, even if it's at the very last second of the arraignment. Do you understand?" Zora nodded. "Good."

His phone vibrated. Silas looked at the message on the screen and stood up. "I have to go. Stay strong, okay?"

"Will do."

"I'll see you later." Then Silas grabbed his brief-case and left.

Zora rested back on the pillow. Her team was

hard at work uncovering the truth, and her job was to stay strong. That she could do.

Besides one more thing.

Zora turned her face and prayed for help to turn the tide in her favor.

33

The young man in the wheelchair looked away from the surging waves that lapped the sand before receding and turned to the older man sitting on the bench beside him. The seagulls squawked overhead, squabbling for morsels of food that the kitchen staff had put out, but the young man paid them no mind.

He pulled the blanket around him tighter as the cool afternoon wind ruffled his hair. "I have to go," he said to the older man. He was certain the older man knew what he was referring to. He must have feared this since he'd flown to the island as soon as he'd heard the young man had woken up.

It'd only been three days since the young man returned to the land of the living, but he'd made speedy recovery, thanks to the care the nurse—she'd said her name was Lila—had given him over the months. And against doctor's orders to take it easy, he'd been pushing himself hard to recover his strength.

Because he needed it for what he was about to do.

"You heard the news," the older man said, rubbing his large hands together.

The young man nodded. They'd tried to keep the news from him, but he'd overhead the old man's conversation on the phone. Finding out the rest had been easy.

The older man let out a sigh. "I'm not sure that's a good idea," he said in a gravelly voice. "You need time to recover."

"It can't wait," the young man stated.

The older man glanced at him. "And what if I tried to stop you?"

The young man looked him straight in the eye, saying nothing in return. There was no need. He was sure the older man knew he couldn't stop him if he wanted.

The older man exhaled. "Alright. But I'm sending people with you. I don't need to emphasize that you need to keep a low profile."

The young man could accept that. "Thank you," he said simply.

Then they turned back to staring at the waves of the aquamarine sea as they crashed on the beach.

34

Silas removed his jacket and flung it at the back of his chair in Adrianna's dining room. The area had become their command center for Zora's case, and now stacks of paper covered most of its surface. Adrianna had even set up a fax and photocopying machine in one corner of the room. AJ had claimed another spot and only left it either to relieve himself, to see Zora at the hospital, or to rest when Adrianna insisted on it. Silas didn't blame him —he would have done the same if the woman he loved was in danger.

Speaking of said woman, where was she?

"She took Sparky out for a brief walk," AJ said, as if reading his thoughts.

Silas liked the one-eyed chihuahua. Sure, the dog

loved to get underfoot, but Sparky was so cute, Silas couldn't imagine a time he'd never been in the family. Adrianna loved to walk him around the estate, but he also knew she used the time to sort through her thoughts alone. He hoped she wasn't too worried about the case. Silas and Adrianna had never lost before, and they had no plans to start now when it really mattered.

He heard the front door open, and Sparky's yaps filled the air. The little rascal scampered across the floor and was soon curled up in his favorite spot under the table. Adrianna strode in, wearing a turtleneck sweater over dark jeans.

"Ugh, it's getting colder," she said, blowing into her hands. "And it's not even November yet."

Though it'd only been two hours since he'd last seen her, Silas couldn't help walking over and giving her a kiss on the cheek. "You look as beautiful as always, my darling," he said.

Zora's mom blushed at his words. Then her face turned serious. "How is she?" she asked.

"Hanging in there. Your daughter is stronger than she looks, just like her mama."

Adrianna smiled. "Thanks for saying that." Then she went into boss mode. "Okay, let's review what we have," she said as she headed over to the dining area and settled into her seat.

"I think we've made some progress on the annotations in Herbert's ledger," AJ said. "Like we suspected, the other acronyms stood for other diagnostic tests used in the hospital."

"By only surgeons?" Adrianna asked.

AJ shook his head. "Across all departments," he replied. "But the surgical units used most of them." He checked his notes. "Herbert also listed the dates when those tests were ordered and by what department. At first, we assumed he'd gotten all the information as part of the network responsible for the fraud, but a further look shows it might not be the case. We didn't find any deposits in Herbert's financial records that matched any of these charges—we could do so for the drug-related entries in his ledger.

"Then Clive worked his magic and got his hands on the detailed hospital records that matched these tests—don't ask me how," AJ continued. "All those tests together translated into a lot of money. We're thinking millions. And we have to believe this is just a tiny subset of what's been going on, though we have no way of verifying that. But what's important to note is that Herbert's name didn't come up in any of those records. So it's safe to assume that Herbert was looking into them as well."

Adrianna rubbed her forehead. "But why would he do that? Wasn't he a part of the group?"

"I don't know," AJ said. "Maybe he was building evidence, something he could use as leverage against the club."

Adrianna leaned back. "But why?"

"I think I have an idea," Silas said. "Helen sent me this information a few minutes ago." Helen was one of Adrianna's longtime employees who worked under Silas. "She looked into the Gentlemen Surgeons Club, and it seems there are two tiers of members: the general members, and then the inner circle made up of a tiny subset of surgeons. If you were Herbert, which group would you want to be a part of?"

"Definitely the inner circle," Adrianna said.

"So if he wasn't one of them already, which we can assume is the case, since he's not involved in the diagnostics fraud, which is where all the big bucks seem to be, then maybe he thinks this information might be his way in," AJ said.

"Correct," Silas said.

"So poor Herbert wasn't part of the inner circle,"

Adrianna said in a cynical tone. "Do you think the inner circle found out and killed him?"

Silas leaned back. "We don't know."

They all mulled over the information for a while.

Then AJ straightened. "We also looked into Herbert's personal life."

"Anything there?" Adrianna asked.

"He was married, but had no kids."

Adrianna's eyes widened. "He didn't strike me as the type. To be married, I mean."

"It seems most people didn't know," AJ said. "They didn't live together, though they spent significant days, sometimes weeks, at each other's place, according to the help."

"So how's the grieving widow?" Silas asked.

AJ shuffled some papers. "We've found nothing out of the ordinary in her daily activities, though we're checking into her background, too."

"What does she do?" Adrianna asked.

"She's a housewife," AJ replied.

Adrianna's eyebrow rose. "Even though she doesn't live with him?"

"Yes, from what I gathered."

AJ leaned forward. "But we found something in her financial records. It appears she received regular monthly deposits from Herbert. However…"

"What?" Silas said.

"There were also periodic payments from another account," AJ said. "From a paper company."

Silas rubbed his jaw. "Interesting. Do we know who owns it?"

AJ shook his head. "We traced it to Cyprus, but that's where we lost the trail."

"Do you think she's having an affair?" Adrianna asked.

"Maybe," Silas said. "Or maybe she was running a business she didn't want anyone to know about. What do you think, AJ?"

"I'm not sure about the business angle," AJ replied. "She doesn't seem the type. But you never know."

"Anyway, let's keep digging there," Adrianna said. "It might be something important. And let me know if you need any help with a background check on the paper company. I have a team that's good at that sort of thing."

"I'll let you know. Thanks," AJ said.

Adrianna leaned back. "Good job, guys," she said.

They were making progress, but Adrianna wondered if they were missing some angle to the case.

35

M adam Sherry lit a cigarette and then turned to her companion, who was still naked under the sheets. The curtains at Alex's apartments were partly closed, and Sherry could tell from the sun's position over the horizon that it was only evening.

"You're playing a dangerous game," Alex said.

She shrugged and took another drag of her cigarette.

Alex sat up. "What if he finds out that you're here? With me?"

She stretched out on the bed and blew a ring toward the ceiling. "He won't."

"How can you be so sure?"

Sherry turned to Alex. "I fooled Herbert all that time, didn't I?"

He rubbed his bare chest. "Herbert was a fool."

"My fool," she breathed. "May his soul rest in peace."

Alex laughed. "Are you for real? You killed him."

"Well, he was unfaithful, even if he was just a client."

Alex looked at her in disbelief. "But aren't you doing the same?"

Why was it so hard for men to understand? "I've always been this way. From the beginning. He, however, wasn't supposed to change."

Then Alex's phone rang. Sherry watched as he answered it. When he finished the conversation, he dropped the phone on the nightstand.

"Who was it?" she asked.

"They need the girls."

She faced the ceiling again and blew out another ring. "I'm not going. I have business to attend to."

"Who said you were? Now, are you going to spend all this time talking? We could be engaging in more productive activities," Alex said, with a twinkle in his eye.

Sherry said nothing and instead blew out one

more ring of smoke and stubbed out the cigarette in the ashtray on the nightstand.

Then she pounced on him.

———

The surgeon drove his car into his garage and felt her presence. She was standing in the shadowed area, right next to the tools section. He closed his garage and then headed to where she waited.

"I couldn't wait to see you," she said. Her alluring perfume wrapped around him, and he fought the urge to inhale.

"I'm glad," he said. "I missed you."

"Me too. But I can't stay. His family is around, and I can't be away for too long. I've waited a while here for you."

"I understand," he said.

She reached forward and gave him a kiss on the cheek. "I'll see you in a few days."

"Alright." Then he pulled her into a hug and kissed her thoroughly. He almost didn't want to let her go, yet he released her.

Then she left.

But the surgeon knew this was the last time he would see her. She'd betrayed him with that sanctimonious bastard—he'd caught them together by chance in the library. They hadn't known he was there.

The surgeon let out a sigh. As much as he loved her, he had to punish her. Punish them for betraying him.

So the surgeon had left the spying bug he'd found in its place.

36

It hadn't surprised Roberts when the others had requested an emergency meeting. Now they were together in the private lounge. Only Allen seemed at ease, which wasn't unusual for him. Allen and Lewis had been the last to arrive.

Lewis began pacing, then stopped and turned to Roberts. "How can Clark be dead? Suicide? Impossible!"

Roberts shrugged. "I don't believe it either. But there was no evidence of foul play."

Hill scoffed. "That means nothing. Any good professional can make a murder look like suicide."

"First Herbert, and now Clark. What's going on?" Lewis said.

"The deaths may not be related," Hill said. "Herbert wasn't a member of our group."

"I think we need to beef up security for all of us," Lewis suggested.

"I'm not sure that's necessary," Roberts said. "But if you want to, why not? I can make the arrangements if we all agree."

"I don't care for the idea of some grunt following me into the bathroom when I need to take a piss," Hill said.

"Me neither," Allen said.

"And I don't think it's necessary," Roberts said, "which means we won't be employing any extra security. Majority rules, as usual."

Lewis' shoulders slumped. The man was not happy with the decision.

"But the real question is: what about Clark's records?" Allen asked. "Will any of it lead back to us?"

The room fell silent. Roberts could imagine their minds racing to see if they'd left any traces of their relationship.

He cleared his throat. All eyes turned to him. "It's been taken care of," he said.

"How?" Hill asked.

"I reached out to Clark's widow and promised her

we'll take care of her. She's already asked the cops to close the case so she can grieve in peace."

"How much?" Lewis asked.

"Thirty million dollars," Roberts replied.

"That should do it," Hill said.

"I'm sure that's much more than she'd hoped for, considering Clark was a stingy bastard," Allen said. Only he could deliver an insult and make it sound like a compliment.

"Anything else?" Roberts asked. No one said a word, but he was certain they'd think more about it when they got home tonight. "Alright, I believe we're good for today."

"So I know this was an emergency meeting," Hill started. "But any chance—"

"They're available," Roberts replied. "I took the liberty of calling them here." He pulled out his phone and pressed a couple of buttons.

The double doors opened, and the bodyguard stepped in and then made way for the girls.

Tiny entered the private lounge and headed to the decorative mask that hung on the wall opposite the floor-to-ceiling windows once the men were all busy with the girls in different bedrooms scattered all over the mansion. He removed it from the wall, slipped his hand behind it, and pulled out the bug he'd inserted there.

Tiny had placed the recording device there on the first day he'd led the girls into this room. He'd waited until they were all occupied, even Alex, who had accompanied them. Then he'd hidden it there. But time was ticking, and he had to retrieve what had been recorded. Tiny hoped it'd be enough.

When Zora had ended up in detention, Tiny hadn't been able to stop it since he'd been out of state. But when they'd arrested Zora this time around, he couldn't let the cycle repeat itself. So he'd taken the first flight back into town. Once he'd returned, Tiny had first gone to the grave of that fool, Thomas Stewart, and desecrated it. A perfect tombstone was too good for him.

Tiny had killed his boss, Drake Pierce, when he'd threatened Zora's life, and he was prepared to do so again to anyone who tried to make her life a living hell. Zora didn't deserve it—she was the embodiment of all that was good and right with this world, just like his sister had been before some gangbangers had gunned her down in a drive-by shooting and his world shattered. Zora had brought back meaning into his life, and if anything happened to her, that meant the world as he knew it no longer had any significance. So for now, Tiny monitored Detective Morris. Tiny wasn't a cop-killer, but he could become one if it came to it.

He'd dug into Herbert's background as soon as he'd arrived and had discovered Herbert had been in a relationship with Madam Sherry. Madam Sherry was connected to Alex, so Tiny had sought employment with him in the hope he'd get close enough to Madam Sherry to find out what had happened with Herbert. That was why he'd planted the bugs.

Tiny had also seen pictures of Herbert's wrapped corpse. Most professionals had unique ways of wrapping a body, especially if they'd been in the business for quite some time. To the normal eye, there was no difference, but Tiny had been in the body and organ business for years, so he knew what to look for. He'd narrowed it down to a pair of goons that worked together. From there, it'd been easy to track them down.

The first, Tommy, had been loyal to the end and had refused to give up the name of the client, but Elvis had sung like a bird, and it hadn't been difficult for Tiny to explain to him what he wanted. It had then taken Tiny some extra digging to find out who had killed Herbert and why—she'd hidden herself well. But he needed concrete evidence if he wanted Zora to be set free. Which was why he was here, retrieving the bugs he'd set up.

Tiny snuck into the library next and headed into the adjoining bedroom. Madam Sherry was not here today, so Tiny assumed the room would be empty. He headed to the nude painting hanging over the massive king-sized bed, brought it down, and removed the bug he'd hidden behind one of the eyes that stared back at him from the painting. Then he replaced the frame on the wall, hurried back into the library, and then slid out before shutting the door.

"What are you doing?"

Tiny whirled to see Alex coming down the winding staircase.

"Madam Sherry asked me to pick up an earring she'd left on the table in the library," Tiny said.

Alex's eyes narrowed. "What earring?" he asked.

Tiny opened his hand to reveal a black pearl earring. It had been a gift from Dr. Roberts to Madam Sherry on her birthday, and it was one of a set that Madam Sherry treasured.

Alex's face cleared. He must have recognized it. "Well, see you don't come near here again. This room is off limits for staff."

"Yes, sir," Tiny said.

"Now get back to the girls."

"Yes, sir," Tiny said and headed back up the stairs. As he passed Alex and continued upward, Tiny could feel his eyes following him all the way.

37

"Dr Martin, Dr. Martin!"

Jason looked up. He'd gotten distracted again. "Sorry, what were you saying, Dr. Lee?" Jason asked his senior surgical resident.

He was on yet another night call in the ER. The place had been like a madhouse all evening and had only settled down. Jason had been updating patient notes at the computer terminal attached to the nursing station when the resident had called his name.

The short resident just smiled patiently. "Mrs. Doolittle has refused to allow the junior residents to set up her IV line. She says she'd like it if you could come hold her hand for it."

"Alright," Jason said. The senior resident left to attend to another patient.

The ER nurses around him snickered. "She has a crush on you, Dr. Martin," one of them said.

"Definitely a crush," another nurse said. "Not that I blame her." The nurses chuckled.

"No wonder she's been visiting the ER more often," a third nurse said. "And she knows we can't turn her away."

Jason ignored them since Mrs. Doolittle, a sweet old lady that reminded him of the grandmother he'd never have, wasn't the reason he'd been distracted.

He couldn't get Dr. Zora Smyth out of his mind.

Jason hadn't been a monk all his life, but he'd never been one for relationships with his previous profession. He hadn't had time for dating either, and it'd never bothered him.

So it was a mystery to him that Dr. Smyth had gotten under his skin.

He couldn't say what about her that had caught his attention, but he had to admit he liked her all the same.

And now she had an arraignment coming up— he'd overhead Valentine gossiping about it. She probably had a legal team in place—Jason had noticed the sharp-looking gentleman with the briefcase, whom he'd assumed was in charge. A little dig into her background had also revealed her mother owned one of the prominent law firms in the city.

But he'd seen people fail even with all that, especially if there was someone pulling the strings in the background. What if she got charged with second degree murder? Dr. Smyth would lose her fellowship spot and any other opportunities that might have come her way, and may never recover from it. She'd have a black mark on her record that would follow her everywhere and affect other open positions she might have benefited from—even if she never got convicted.

All for a crime he didn't think she committed.

No one was foolish enough, and definitely not Dr. Smyth, to store a body in their car and have it waiting in the trunk for them after a flight. Especially not with Herbert's sketchy dealings to consider. A probe here and there, nothing special that would draw attention to Jason, had shown the guy had run with the wrong crowd and was knee deep in the kind of trouble that gave doctors everywhere a bad name. Not that Jason was a paragon of innocence, but his deals had been sanctioned and thus considered legal.

And now time was running out for Dr. Smyth.

Jason let out a breath. He couldn't let things continue this way.

There was one thing he could do.

It was a risk and could ruin the plan he'd laid in place.

But doing nothing for Dr. Smyth was no longer an option. His conscience wouldn't allow it, however shriveled it might be.

With his mind made up, Jason logged out of the computer terminal and headed to Mrs. Doolittle's cubicle to hold her hand.

38

Adrianna, Silas, and AJ sat around the dining table on Sunday evening and ran through all the information they'd collected so far. Alisa hadn't joined them since she had to work on a large corporate case.

A tense silence filled the air.

Then Adrianna sighed. "I don't think this is going to be enough," she said.

"I know," AJ said. "But we can't let them charge Zora with murder."

Silas' lips settled into a grim line. "We won't," he promised.

Adrianna ran a hand over her hair. This time, she was scared. "But how?" She closed her eyes and let out an exhale. "I can't let anything happen to my baby."

Silas came over to her side and wrapped her in a hug. "We won't let them have her."

Adrianna rested her head against his torso. Silas was her wall of strength—he'd stuck by her side through every trouble and was always there to support her. "I know she's keeping up a brave front for now, but I can't watch her crumble again. Her last time in detention almost killed her."

AJ straightened. "We can't give up yet." He rifled through the stacks of paper in front of him.

"What are you doing?" Silas asked.

"Looking for anything we might have missed," AJ said as he continued to examine the documents. Then he looked up. "But I'm still hopeful we'll find a video footage that showed who dumped the body and who made the deposit at the ATM."

Silas released Adrianna. "Helen thinks she might have something for us on that front by morning, though it looks like a wild shot," he said. Helen was a trusted employee who'd come through for them multiple times in the past. Adrianna prayed she'd do the same again.

She let out an exhale. "We need a miracle."

The doorbell chimed throughout the house.

Adrianna looked from Silas to AJ. "Who can that be?" she said.

"No idea," Silas said. "I'm not expecting anyone. Our people would have just called."

"Definitely not for me," AJ said.

They turned in the entrance's direction as Alisa poked her head into the dining area. "Mom, Silas, there's someone here to see you."

"Me too?" Silas asked.

"Yes," Alisa said. "He asked for you by name. Says it's about Zora."

"Who is it?" AJ asked.

"A Dr. Jason Martin," Alisa said. "He says he's Zora's colleague."

39

Ethan leaned forward in the swivel chair and listened to the individual on the other end of the burner phone he kept on his person.

"Thanks," he said. "I owe you one." Then he ended the call.

He tapped his fingers on the conference table in the radiologists' lounge, grateful that none of the other doctors had arrived this early on Monday morning.

Ethan had thought he had a few more weeks before it was time to leave, but it seemed the long arm of the law was groping after him, and Ethan had no desire to be anyone's fall guy. His only regret was he didn't have time to say goodbye to Christina, since she hadn't arrived yet—Ethan liked to get in early to review his work before the day started.

But maybe it was for the best. She'd started avoiding him, and Ethan had guessed Molly was the reason why—he'd experienced similar when Molly had done the same to other ladies Ethan had shown interest in before.

Thankfully, he'd prepared for this day. He got up, packed up his research materials from the table, and moved them to the locker. Then he grabbed an envelope, which he tucked into his medical coat, and secured the locker. This was the last time he was ever going to need any of those things.

Then he stepped out of the room.

"Where are you going?"

Ethan turned to see Molly standing a few feet away with a spray bottle and cleaning rags in her hands. Why was she here? He forced himself to remain calm. He had to be careful not to give away his plans. Fortunately, he'd had lots of experience in hiding his true feelings. "Just got paged about one of my patients who ended up in the ER. Want to come along?"

Molly wrinkled her nose in disgust. "No, thanks," she said. Just like he'd expected. Molly hated the sight of blood.

"Okay, I'll see you later."

"Sure." She watched him until the elevator doors closed.

Ethan let out a sigh of relief as the elevator headed down to the ground floor. When the doors opened, he waited a few seconds and then pressed the button for the parking level, where he made a brief stop before taking it back up to the ground floor.

He got off and hurried through the ER until he arrived at its entrance. Then he quickly approached the first cab parked at the cab stand and slipped in. "Central Station please," he said.

The taxi driver nodded and took off even as Ethan removed his medical coat. Given the hour of the day, they soon arrived at the train station. Ethan paid cash to the driver and hopped out. "Keep the change," he said. The driver thanked him and sped away.

Ethan hurried into the station and reached the locker he'd secured many months ago. The place was teeming with people headed in all directions, just the way Ethan preferred. He opened the locker and grabbed the backpack, as well as the change of clothing he'd kept in there. Then he slammed the locker shut.

He strode to the restroom and changed out of his scrubs, then donned his new outfit and a pair of black glasses he'd retrieved from the side pocket of his backpack. Ethan was now James Winston, a thirty-two-year-old business consultant from Boston. He flushed the IDs from his old life down the toilet and then dumped the coat and scrubs in the bin.

Ethan hurried out and caught the next train headed to a station near the airport terminal.

An hour later, he was airborne on a connecting flight to London on his way to begin his new life.

40

The rest of the weekend had passed quietly for Zora. Silas, Zora's mom, and AJ had spent all Sunday tracking down every lead and clue they had, yet nothing had panned out. Still, they hadn't given up and had taken turns coming by to spend time with her. By the time Zora had settled in for the night, they'd been no closer to the truth than when they'd started the day.

Then Monday morning dawned bright and sunny. The new judge had decided to hold the arraignment in the hospital, so the hospital staff had arrived early to set up the place. They'd tightened security on the VIP floor, and the nurses had their hands full keeping the press away.

Christina's friend, the nurse who'd helped drive

away the detectives, came by and helped Zora be as presentable as she could. Soon the judge, the court clerk, who was there to record the proceedings, the prosecution, and the defense arrived in the hospital room.

As the proceedings were about to start, a member of the prosecutor's team entered and whispered something to the ADA. The ADA glanced at him sharply, then his eyes flickered to the defense team for a moment.

Zora's curiosity piqued. What had the man told him? With the way his eyes had darted to Silas, Zora believed whatever information he'd received had bearing on the case. Then she noticed one of Silas' associates showing Silas something on his phone. If Zora had to hazard a guess, Silas had just received the same information, because he glanced at the ADA.

Then the hearing began. Silas stated for the record that he was appearing on behalf of Dr. Zora Smyth, who was present on the hospital bed.

Judge Weston, who could pass for a doctor with his tall frame, salt-and-pepper hair, and wire-rimmed glasses, dispensed with the preliminaries. The ADA stepped forward. Silas had mentioned the ADA, who looked deceptively young with the flick of dark hair covering his forehead, was gunning to be the next DA. "Smart" and "sharp" were the words Silas had used.

The ADA stated they'd charged Zora with second degree murder. Then the judge asked Silas if he wanted to be heard on the motions he'd filed.

"Your Honor," Silas began, "we're filing a motion, requesting that the charges filed against Dr. Zora Smyth be dismissed."

"Counsel, what's the state's position?" Judge Weston asked the prosecutor.

Zora let out a sigh of relief. Silas had cautioned that the judge might decide not to hear the motion at this hearing.

"Your Honor, we ask that the motion be dismissed. We have evidence to prove the defendant was responsible for the death of Dr. Herbert Johnson."

Zora glared at the prosecutor. Did he mean the fake evidence?

Judge Weston turned to Silas. "What do you have to say to that?"

"Your Honor," Silas began, "the evidence the prosecution is referring to is shaky at best. The witness' testimony, on which this whole case rests, is not reliable since the witness has since retracted his statement."

The judge glanced at the ADA. "Counsel, is that true? Did the witness' testimony change?"

The ADA's mouth tightened. "Yes, Your Honor. However, we have other corroborating evidence which we're looking forward to presenting at trial."

One of Silas' investigators leaned forward and showed Silas something on his phone.

"Your Honor, we have a video showing that the evidence the prosecution has is all a setup," Silas said.

Zora saw the judge's eyes light up with interest. *Please, please, allow them to show you the video*, she prayed.

"Objection, Your Honor," the ADA said. "The defense can present that at trial."

The judge thought for a moment. "I'll allow it," he finally said. "I'm assuming we can all see the video."

"Your Honor!" the ADA said. "We don't know if said video is fake."

The judge scowled at him. "We won't know until we see the video. I'll make that judgment, counsel."

Yes! Zora wanted to cheer, but she kept her face impassive, the perfect picture of innocence.

It seemed Silas' team had prepared for this eventuality, because they rolled in a large mobile screen and cast the video on the phone onto it.

Zora studied the screen as the video played out. It showed the back of two men dumping a wrapped package in the trunk of a car. As they stepped back, Zora could see the car's license plate. It was her car!

"Your Honor, that is the license plate of my client's car. And my client was on a flight from Europe at that time," Silas commented.

Zora wasn't sure if Silas should have said that. They wouldn't be able to refute it as evidence later if the judge ended up dismissing the motion and allowing the case to go to trial. But maybe he had a reason for this.

Her eyes swung back to the video. At the last minute, one of the men turned, and the camera caught his full face. Silas froze that view.

"Your Honor, this man, also known as Elvis, is the so-called witness the prosecution planned to use."

The judge cocked an eyebrow. "Counsel, is that true?"

"Your Honor, this is the first time we're seeing this video," the ADA said. "And even with this, the cops caught Dr. Smyth driving with a body in her trunk. In addition, there is still evidence that Dr.

Smyth transferred fifty thousand dollars from her account to an account associated with criminal activity."

"Your Honor," Silas said. "the transferred amount is not a direct evidence of the crime in question. And there's no linkage to my client's so-called accomplice, who seems to not exist."

"Counsel, does the state have evidence linking the account to the accomplice in question?"

The ADA fidgeted. "Not at this time, Your Honor. But if you give us a few days, we'll have it."

"Your Honor, the prosecution has had more than enough time to dig into the life of the so-called accomplice and even the witness," Silas said. His associate handed him a sheet of paper and a photo, both of which he scanned quickly. "The so-called witness is a known criminal with a long list of crimes, which puts into question his reliability, especially now that we know he lied about his role in the crime. In addition, we've just gotten a photo from a video recorded by a car in the area that showed Elvis was the one who deposited the fifty thousand dollars into Dr. Smyth's account. We have a statement from Dr. Smyth's bank that confirms the time the transaction was made."

"Let me see the documents," the judge said. Silas handed them over to him.

The judge examined them for a few minutes. "Counsel, have you seen these?" he finally said.

"No, Your Honor," the ADA said. The judge passed them over to him, and Zora saw his face tighten as his eyes swept over them. "Your Honor, the defense is welcome to bring all their evidence to court at the trial. But this hearing is not the right forum for it."

"Okay," the judge said. "I think I've heard enough for now."

Zora's heart sank. She could sense it hadn't been enough, and even the ADA's face said as much. But then she saw AJ whispering into Silas' ear.

"Your Honor, there's also some breaking news that's coming through right now about the actual killer that impacts this case," Silas said.

The judge narrowed his eyes at Silas. "Counsel, I think we've had enough for today."

"Please, Your Honor," Silas said. "It won't take more than a minute."

"On TV?"

"Objection, Your Honor," the ADA said. "Whatever that news is, it's irrelevant to this hearing."

The judge leaned forward and thought for a

moment. It seemed like hours to Zora. She prayed the whole time.

"Put it on," the judge said.

"Your Honor!" the ADA protested.

"I'd like to see what it is before I make my judgement."

Zora's shoulders sank with relief. Silas motioned to AJ, and he switched on Zora's hospital TV and scrolled until he found what he was looking for.

A dark-skinned female reporter was speaking in front of what looked like a grand estate. "I'm standing here in front of the Gaytinson mansion, which is the present location of the Gentlemen Surgeons Club, an old-boys club for elite surgeons from Lexinbridge Regional Hospital. We've just received information that the FBI has launched a massive investigation into this organization on counts of healthcare fraud involving diagnostic tests, prescriptions drugs, and therapies.

"We've also learned that Dr. Johnson and Dr. Clark, who both passed away recently, were members of this club, and there are speculations they were murdered to cover up this organization's crimes. In addition, according to an FBI anonymous source, Dr. Johnson's wife, Cindy Johnson, was having an affair with the leader of the organization, a Dr. Roberts, both of whom are now suspects in the murder of Dr. Johnson. More information to come even as the investigations continue." The screen switched to another setting, and AJ turned the TV off.

"I think I've heard and seen enough," the judge said. "Counsel, do you have anything else to add?"

"Not at this time, Your Honor," the ADA said.

"So here's my judgement. The court does not find probable cause to believe the defendant committed the crime. Therefore, I order the release of Dr. Zora Smyth." He turned to the ADA. "Counsel, you're welcome to file new charges against the defendant once you have more evidence. Mr. Parks, I don't believe there's any need for the second motion anymore, correct?"

"Yes, Your Honor," Silas replied.

"This court is adjourned," the judge said.

Zora felt lighter, like a weight had rolled off her shoulders.

Her team had done it. She was finally free.

The hospital room emptied. Soon it was only Zora, her mom, Silas, and AJ present in the room. Even the associates from her mom's law firm had left.

"I'm glad that's over," Zora said.

"Me too," her mom said as she sat beside her on the bed and gave her a hug.

"You need to reward the associates. They worked so hard."

"They already have my card to go out on the town tonight." Her mom released her. "I'm pretty sure I'll get a hefty bill."

Zora turned to Silas and AJ. "Thank you so much. I'm not sure how I can repay you for everything."

"I'll think of something," AJ said. "I'm sure Silas will get his reward from your mom. Ouch! That hurts." He glared at Silas.

"That's what you get for running your mouth in front of your elders," Silas said.

AJ turned to Zora as he rubbed his arm. "It really hurts."

Zora chuckled. "You deserved it." She looked from him to Silas and her mom. "FBI investigation, huh?"

"It wasn't any of us," AJ said.

"Really? Who then?"

"A certain doctor," Silas said. "Dr. Martin."

Zora's eyes widened. Who would have thought? She hadn't spoken to him since the day she'd driven him away. "How?"

"He showed up in front of the house last night," Silas said. "It seems he'd done some digging of his own. I'm not sure how he did it, but he had reams of information on the club and suggested we send it to the FBI. Said we could just claim it landed on our doorstep, which was really where he dropped the box off."

"We went through the information all night and this morning," her mom continued. "That was why we couldn't come and see you before the arraignment. Then Silas called a friend at the FBI, and we gave him everything we'd gathered and what Dr. Martin had dropped off. And he took over from there."

Then Silas' phone rang. He pulled it out, answered, and then listened. "Okay, good to hear," he finally said. "Have a good weekend." Then he ended the call.

"Who was it?" Zora's mom asked.

"That was the ADA," Silas said. "The DA's office has decided to drop the charges against Zora."

Zora couldn't help the smile that filled her face. She blinked back the tears that suddenly rushed to her eyes. She was really free. Finally.

Her mom pulled her into a hug. "Thank God."

AJ grinned from ear to ear. "That's awesome news."

Her mom released her, and Zora leaned back. It was almost too incredible to believe.

"But that was quick," her mom said. "I thought they'd take a day before making the decision."

"Give me one second to find out what happened," Silas said.

He made a call, listened, and then ended the call. Then he turned to them. "It seems the mayor put some pressure on him."

Zora furrowed her forehead. "The mayor? What does he have to do with anything in this case?" She'd saved his daughter's life a while back, and his help had ended up aiding Zora in one of her previous cases.

"Well, it turns out his daughter gave him a hard time about it, and he in turn put pressure on the DA's office."

Zora chuckled. "Wow!" She would never have thought the patient remembered her. But she was grateful for her support. She'd find a way later to say her thanks.

Then something occurred to her. "What about the whole affair thing on TV? That was a surprise."

Her mom looked at the others. "It wasn't from either of us."

"And then the whole witness statement retraction," AJ said. "That was unexpected."

"I wonder what made him change his mind," Zora said.

It was bizarre indeed, but she was grateful for whatever had elicited that change, since it had begun the process of getting her free.

41

Tiny stared at the TV screen in the tiny but clean room he'd called home for the past few weeks. The news had just broken that the DA's office had dropped the charges against Dr. Zora Smyth.

His job here was done.

An email to the right reporter with an attached copy of the video recordings of Madam Sherry and Dr. Roberts, plus a picture of the woman in question with Herbert, had been enough. The press would have much to talk about in the coming months. He'd also given Elvis a nudge in the right direction.

Tiny picked up his duffel bag. It was time for his shift at Alex's business, but he wasn't going back there.

It was time for him to leave.

He stepped out of his room, closed the door behind him, and disappeared into the shadows.

42

The woman sat in her office, playing with the knife as she stared at the screen.

It was all over.

After all the years of playing her dangerous little game, she'd finally cut herself.

She let out a chuckle that soon turned into sobs, and she let herself cry for a few minutes. Then she took a deep breath and let out an exhale.

She'd only wanted to belong. Was it so bad that she'd desired a place among society's elite?

The woman had thought Herbert could give her that. She'd regarded him as a client that would help her achieve her dreams, but maybe he'd been even more. The woman had tolerated his quirks and kept him happy. She'd had high hopes for him, but he'd failed miserably. And only when she'd lost all hope with him had she sought a new patron. Who could blame her for that, when she'd given everything and gotten nothing in return?

But Herbert had found out and had been furious. He'd ranted and raved and had wanted to destroy everything. But she couldn't allow that. It would destroy her dream, after all.

So she'd taken one of his drugs—he'd boasted all the time about its effects—and injected him with it while he slept. Then she'd hired the muscle to get rid of his body.

But they'd botched the job and dumped it in Zora Smyth's car instead.

Zora Smyth. Oh, how she hated her. Herbert was always complaining about her, and she'd only thought it was petty jealousy.

Until she saw him that day.

Herbert hadn't known she was awake. She'd gotten up in the middle of the night to use the bathroom, only to find him pleasuring himself and ejaculating over Zora's picture.

She'd realized he was obsessed with Zora Smyth and mad that he couldn't have her and understood Zora was the only one he'd loved all along.

A part of her heart had died that day, and that was

when she'd sought a new man with power and prestige like Dr. Roberts. Well, two if one included the quiet surgeon, Dr. Allen. She'd vowed she'd never make the same mistake again. No one man deserved her whole heart.

So she found it ironic when his body ended up in Zora's car. Then, to teach the goons a lesson—because she'd never let such a mistake go unpunished—and to rope Zora further into the case, she'd ordered Elvis to make a witness statement. She'd even paid someone to beat her to death in lockup. Everything had gone well until it hadn't.

And now it was all over.

The woman couldn't run—she promised herself she'd never do that even if she lost the game. She was a person who took responsibility seriously.

A knock sounded on her door, and her maid poked her head in. She was one of the loyal ones—the other servants had fled as soon as the news broke.

"Ma'am," she said in that familiar, timid voice. "The cops are here to see you."

She nodded. It was time.

She got up and adjusted her dress until she was satisfied. There was nothing wrong with looking good while going out in a blaze of shame.

Then she stepped out of her office and into the living room.

A detective thrust a warrant in her face. From the corner of her eye, she could see the flashes of the cameras going off outside, and she smiled at the ridiculousness of everything.

"Mrs. Cindy Johnson, you're under arrest for the murder of your husband, Dr. Herbert Johnson."

Her mind tuned out everything else the detective said.

Then they cuffed her and led her away.

43

Tommy stood on the riverbank next to the man, whose limbs were as wide as tree trunks. They both stared across the river at the city of Lexinbridge, all lit up in its dark glory.

"Why did you let me live?" Tommy asked after a while.

The man stayed silent at first. "Because you were loyal to the end," he said. Then he shot Tommy a dark look. "But make no mistake. Your life now belongs to me."

Tommy knew better than to contradict the man. "Yes, sir."

"You'll need to disappear for a while," the man said.

Tommy had guessed that—he'd already bought

his bus ticket out of town. He'd go to his sister's place in Kentucky. She and her husband had a farm there. It would be a big change, but Tommy was no stranger to hard work. And maybe it would do him some good. A close brush with death could do that to a man.

Elvis probably thought Tommy was dead. Well, Tommy'd had no choice but to leave him to fight his own battles. In the end, it was every man for himself.

But how would Tommy know when the man needed him? When it was time?

He turned to ask the man, but he was gone, and only Tommy remained standing there.

Tommy took one last look at the city.

Then he turned and walked away.

EPILOGUE

The young man stepped down from the private jet that had brought him back to Lexinbridge and inhaled the cool evening air.

He'd missed this city. It was good to be home.

He was still unsteady on his feet, so he had to use a cane for now. But he expected he wouldn't need it after a few weeks.

Now that his feet had touched the soils of Lexinbridge, he couldn't wait to see her again.

The man straightened and strode toward the airport terminal as fast as the cane and his body would let him, his bodyguards hurrying behind him like shadows in the wind.

They'd gathered back at her mom's home that evening to celebrate. Zora's mom, Silas, AJ, Alisa, and even Brian and Christina. All her friends and family in one place. Except Clive, who had a previous appointment he had to make.

She smiled as AJ and Silas fought over who was in charge of the barbecue pit. They'd decided to celebrate outside before it became too cold. Thankfully, the weather had cooperated. Zora didn't know what was going on with those two, but she was glad they'd found their own rhythm and ways of getting along.

Her sister and her mom were indoors in the kitchen putting together platters of food. They'd barred Zora and Christina from helping, so now they sat next to each other on the porch, with Brian on the other side of Christina, staring at AJ's antics.

"I didn't know he was that mischievous," Christina said. "He's good for you."

Zora took a sip of her punch. "He's just a friend." Her heart was still too raw to let anyone else in. But AJ had proven to be a good friend, and she was grateful for that.

"How are you feeling?" Brian asked.

Zora gave him a small smile. "Tired. I feel like I need a long nap."

"I'm sure you do," Brian said. "It's been a stressful couple of days. Are you still having the headaches?" The attending, Dr. Valentine, had signed off on her discharge only a few hours ago. She'd never been happier than when she crossed the threshold and entered her childhood home again.

"Not really," Zora said. "I'm sure it'll fade away in no time." Then she faced both of them. "When are we hearing wedding bells?"

Brian and Christina shared a knowing smile.

"We thought you'd never ask," Christina said. "We hadn't brought it up because of what happened to Dave, but we wanted you to be the first to know."

"Christina and I plan to get married in the spring," Brian said.

Zora's heart swelled with joy. "Congratulations! Is it going to be here or in Boston?"

"Here," Christina said. "Mom is coming into town. She and my godmother—AKA your mom— will handle everything on our behalf. Otherwise, Brian's family will take over the whole wedding. Your mom will take my views into account. Brian's parents are great, but they have all these societal traditions they'll want to include. Aunt Adrianna would be an excellent gatekeeper for that, and her reputation precedes her. They've just been waiting for us to tell them when."

"Just remember to rein in my mom when needed," Zora cautioned.

"Not a problem," Christina said.

Zora listened for a moment. "I think I can hear my mom calling us in." She cupped her hands around her lips. "AJ and Silas, you can stop playing now!" she called out.

They both turned and grinned at her. Then they waved.

An hour later, they were all seated in the living room. On the couches, loveseats, and even on the rug. Dinner had been delicious, and even Silas' barbecued steak had turned out great. Now they were just relaxing and hanging out.

"So, did I tell you I sued the police department like I promised?" Zora's mom said.

"You did?" Christina said.

It didn't surprise Zora. Her mom was a woman of her word. She felt sorry for whomever had received the lawsuit notice. Zora was sure heads would roll. Not that she cared; they'd made her life miserable enough for the past couple of years.

She glanced at Silas, who was beaming at her

mom with pride, and she chuckled. *Lawyers! The things that excited them.*

Zora took a sip of coffee. She needed a break. "I've been thinking…"

Her mom turned to her. "What, dear?"

"I might work at a different hospital after I finish my fellowship."

"Outside Lexinbridge?" her mom asked, a hint of worry in her voice.

Zora smiled at her to allay her fears. "Maybe. I'm still thinking about it."

"That's a great idea," AJ said. Zora beamed her gratitude at his support. "A change of scenery might do her good."

"But—"

Silas held her mom close and kissed her head. "Zora will be alright regardless of her decision," he said. "We'll just make sure we're here for her, no matter what. Like always."

"Yes, we will," her mom said and then gave Zora a small smile.

Zora returned her smile. Her mom wanted her close, no doubt. Zora was blessed to have her family and friends here for her, but she needed to make the right decision for herself. For now, it was still an idea.

"Thank you so much for everything," she said. "For always being there for me."

"We love you too, Zora," Christina said, her eyes shiny with tears.

"I promise to be good from now on," Zora said.

"Like that would happen," Alisa murmured under her breath. Zora placed her mug down and rose to her feet. "What?"

Her mom leaned toward Alisa. "I believe that's your cue to run."

"Oh no!" Alisa jumped to her feet and took off around the living room. "Someone, help me!"

Zora raced to catch her. "You should watch your mouth instead."

Alisa ducked just as Zora was about to grab her by the neck. "That's what siblings are for," she grumbled. Then she lifted her hands in surrender. "I'm sorry, I'm sorry!"

Zora caught her, looped a hand around Alisa's neck, and tickled her.

"Ah! I said I was sorry!" Alisa protested. "Please. Please!"

"Okay, for the sake of present company, I'll let you go." Zora released her.

"You're mean," Alisa said.

Zora raised an eyebrow as she settled back into her seat. "You didn't know?"

"Alright, alright. Calm down, girls," her mom said.

Zora lifted her mug and took another sip of her coffee. "So, Christina, did you ever find out who vandalized your car?"

"No," Christina replied. "But I found an envelope filled with forty thousand dollars stuck under the windshield wiper of my rented car."

"That's crazy!" Zora said.

"I know," Christina said. "I'd never seen that kind of money all together in one place. There was a typed note inside that said, 'I'm sorry, Christina,' so I know the money was for me."

"Wow! That's insane. So what do you plan to do with the money?" Zora asked.

"I won't tell. It's a secret."

Zora laughed. "I can't wait."

"Zora, what about your car?" AJ asked.

"They sent a message for Zora to pick it up tomorrow," her mom said. "Zora, do you mind if I scrap the car? I'm not sure how you feel about driving a car that had a dead body in it."

Yes, that would be morbid, Zora thought. "You're welcome to do whatever you want with it," she said.

She'd put her trust fund to good use and buy another car. A new beginning.

Zora lifted her mug for a toast. "To new beginnings."

The room raised theirs too. "To new beginnings!"

The doorbell chimed.

Zora's eyes darted to the door. Who could it be at this hour? "I'll get it," she said and rose to her feet.

She padded through the living room and into the foyer. Then she tapped the security camera and gasped at the face that filled the screen.

Zora's body trembled. It couldn't be.

"Zora, what is it?" Christina must have heard her and came to see what was going on.

But Zora couldn't speak. It had to be an apparition. He was supposed to be dead and buried six feet under.

Christina's eyes flashed with concern. "Hey, girl-friend, what's going on?"

Zora could only point at the camera.

Christina leaned forward to look at the screen and screamed. "Marcus?"

"Come on in."

Morris entered the office to see Captain standing with his back to him.

Captain turned and waved him to a chair. "Sit," he said.

Morris perched on the edge of the seat. Something told him he was in for some bad news. "You called to see me?" he asked.

"Yes." Captain settled in behind his desk. "I have some good news and some bad news."

"Can we start with the good news?"

"Good call," Captain said. "The Zora Smyth case has been closed."

"But—"

"We both know it's over," Captain stated.

"So, what's the bad news?"

"Unfortunately, the guys upstairs have placed you on suspension and on a three-month leave."

Morris' face blanched. "Why?"

"You went on a witch hunt, Morris, which is what I told you not to do, and now we're being sued."

"Sued? By Dr. Smyth?"

"Yes, by her lawyers. And believe me, no one ever wants to be sued by them—they are well known in town as a mean bunch. They named you in the lawsuit." Captain fiddled with a pen. "Because of you, the station has been embarrassed and our name dragged through the mud in the press. So sending you on leave isn't such a hardship, right?" He leaned forward and gave Morris a sad smile. "Maybe this would be a good time to relax and get used to Lexinbridge again, and our way of doing things."

Morris said nothing. He'd had enough humiliation.

Jason opened the door to his apartment and noticed someone had disturbed the short piece of thread he'd always left at the door.

An intruder had been inside his place.

The person had tried to be careful, which meant he was very good. Still, Jason had noticed the difference.

He wasn't surprised they'd found him. Jason had called in a favor to get the information on the Gentlemen Surgeons Club, and it must have set off a trigger.

If they weren't already waiting for him in the apartment, then they'd be back soon.

Of course, the easiest thing to do was disappear and start somewhere else all over again. But there was no point in running again. Jason was tired of it.

This was his home, and he now had a reason to stay. Even if he left, they would go after Dr. Smyth, since she seemed to be his weakness. It wasn't true. Yet.

Jason had heard the stories, though she hadn't told him, of the other guys in her life who had left. Of what she'd suffered in the hands of psychopaths and the law.

There was something about her that spoke to him, to the person he wanted to be.

So Jason couldn't let it happen to her again. Like it had before. He would protect her, no matter what.

He would stay and fight.

For her.

So he moved without a sound, shut the door behind him, and picked up the emergency bag he'd stashed in a hidden panel at the back of the coat closet. Then he padded to a corner of the living room that gave him a clear view of the apartment and its exits.

And settled in to wait.

———————

Thank you so much for reading!

Want to know what happens next to Dr. Jason Martin
& Dr. Zora Smyth?
You can grab THE DOCTOR SPY at
https://dobicross.com

If you've loved reading LETHAL RETRACTION,
Dobi would be grateful if you could spend a few
minutes to leave a review (as short as you like) on the
book's page on your favorite retailer. Your review
would help bring it to the attention of other readers.
Thank you very much.

Check out all Dobi Cross books at https://
dobicross.com

Writing a book is harder and more rewarding than I could have ever imagined. And it would not have been possible without the support, love, and encouragement from my number one cheerleader, my dearest mom. My life would never have been this awesome and wonderful without you.

Of course, I have to thank my precious little DC for his smiles and antics. You brighten my day and give me the strength to keep pushing through.

Thank you to my sisters for encouraging me on this wonderful journey. And a special thanks to my baby brother (who is so not a baby anymore) for being super supportive and checking in on my progress. You guys are the best.

Thank you to my wonderful author friends. You know who you are. Your selflessness and willingness to share what you know has made my writing journey smoother and an exciting one. And a special thanks to Lisa and Deanna whose support have made a difference.

Most of all, I want to thank God who gave me life, surrounded me with the most wonderful people, and loved me all the way. You make my life complete.

And finally, a special thanks to all my readers whose love of my stories spur me on to write more. Thank you!

ABOUT THE AUTHOR

As a former physician and business executive in another life—with a childhood filled with reading multi-genre novels (including Shakespeare in the original version)—Dobi Cross loves to write thrilling stories with heart.

She enjoys dreaming up everyday characters who rise above unfavorable circumstances to overcome incredible odds. When not writing, Dobi can be found binging K-dramas and ice cream with her little sidekick by her side.

Lethal Retraction is the sixth book in the Dr. Zora Smyth Medical Thriller Series. Sign up at https://dobicross.com to be notified when the next Dobi Cross book comes out!

Thanks for reading LETHAL RETRACTION!

9 781958 987131